Things We Nearly Knew

Jim Powell

Things We Nearly Knew

PICADOR

First published 2018 by Picador
an imprint of Pan Macmillan
20 New Wharf Road, London N1 9RR
Associated companies throughout the world
www.panmacmillan.com

ISBN 978-1-5098-4242-1

1 3 5 7 9 8 6 4 2

A CIP catalogue record for this book is available from the British Library.

Typeset by Ellipsis, Glasgow
Printed and bound by CPI Group (UK) Ltd, Croydon, CR0 4YY

Visit **www.picador.com** to read more about all our books
and to buy them. You will also find features, author interviews and
news of any author events, and you can sign up for e-newsletters
so that you're always first to hear about our new releases.

for Kay

1

Arlene came from Pittsburgh. At least, that's my provisional opinion. It's one of the many things about Arlene that remain uncertain. I asked her a few times, like we all did, and never got an answer. Not a direct answer. 'I come from somewhere out there,' she said on one occasion. Don't we all?

At first I thought Arlene came from New York. I had that fixed in my mind before there was any debate on the matter. Thick black hair, slightly waved, just off the shoulder. Red lipstick, nail varnish. Slinky dresses, curving round her backside like the ones my mother used to wear sometimes, when I was growing up, when we were all growing up. That said New York to me. What the hell do I know? I've never been to New York. Come to think of it, neither had my mother.

'That's not coming from New York,' Steve said later. 'That's wanting people to think you come from New York. That's what you do when all you know of New York is what you saw in a magazine when you were a little girl.'

Steve didn't think that Arlene came from Pittsburgh. He thought she was a small town girl from . . . well, I don't know where from. By then it was immaterial because Arlene had gone. Gone for the last time, I mean. She left a few times over the course of the nine months that we knew her, or thought we knew her. Every time could have been the last time.

I was on my own behind the bar when she first came in. It was more than a year ago now, sometime in February, must have been. It was a Monday for certain, because Steve wasn't there. Steve helps me run the place in the evenings. He has Mondays off: those are the nights he reminds himself what his wife looks like. I don't remember who else was there. None of the regulars anyhow. Not Nelson, who would soon come to fancy his chances with Arlene. Not Davy, likewise. Not Mike, who would have been more than interested if he was ten years younger and hadn't got religion. In fact, none of the ones who pay my bills and keep me in cheap cigars. Whoever was there, I'm sure we looked up when she walked in. Anyone would, and not only the men. Arlene would have expected nothing less.

'Vodka Martini,' she said, then told me how to make it the way she liked it, in case I didn't know, which I didn't. We don't have much call for cocktails round here.

To begin with, I expected her to be expecting someone. I didn't ask because you don't, or not at once. I thought she'd take her drink to a distant table and wait.

2

Instead, she sat on a bar stool, one leg crossed over the other, like blondes do in Hollywood movies, and other women you want to talk to and regret later that you did. It crossed my mind that Arlene might once have been a hooker, and in fact the idea has never altogether left my mind. On the other hand, you could have put her in a lounge on Fifth Avenue and she wouldn't have looked out of place. Maybe that's saying the same thing.

Most women are ill at ease in a bar on their own, in my experience. Few attempt it. Arlene looked like she belonged on her own. She didn't seem to expect anyone to speak to her. She appeared not to mind that the customers went on talking to each other. Which isn't to say that she was ignored. While she was there, I'm sure she was the focus of every thought. Once she left, she'd be the focus of every conversation. Arlene would have known that, and it must have been satisfaction enough. After a while, when no one had turned up to meet her, and when she showed no signs of leaving, I spoke to her.

'Passing through town?' I asked.

'I'm not sure right now. I expect I'll be staying for a while.' She reached her arm across the counter. 'My name's Arlene.'

That tickled me. It was the formality of the hand-shake, like we were being introduced at a glitzy ball. But it wasn't formal, because she never said her surname.

It was Mitchell, by the way. We only discovered that

3

lately. It was written in small letters inside her left shoe. Of course, it could have been someone else's shoe.

'Hello, Arlene,' I said. 'Welcome to the best bar in town. Are you from round here?'

'From round abouts,' she said. 'I'm from many places, actually. I think we all are, don't you?'

'No. I'm from one place. Here. Definitely.'

'Born and raised?'

'That's right,' I said. 'Soldered to the town from birth.'

Arlene absorbed this information. 'I'm looking for someone called Jack,' she said. 'He's from these parts. Name mean anything to you?'

Darned stupid question, if you ask me. It's not a large town, but big enough to accommodate a few dozen Jacks, I'd imagine.

'Jack who?'

'I don't know.'

That was a load of help.

'I've known plenty of Jacks,' I said. 'So has everyone. It's not much to go on.'

'I know,' said Arlene. 'I think the one I'm looking for used to live in this town.'

'You don't seem very sure.'

'I'm not.'

'The only Jack I can think of who used to drink here,' I said, trying to be helpful, 'was Jack Nightingale. He's dead, or at least I think he's dead.'

'When did he die?'

'I don't know. Five or six years ago, maybe.'

'Not him, then. My Jack was alive three years ago. And his surname doesn't begin with N. It begins with . . . well, I'm not sure. H, I think. Maybe R. It was hard to tell from the writing.'

'What writing?'

Arlene ignored the question.

'Doesn't matter,' she said. 'It was a long shot. But I'll hang around here a while, if it's the same to you.'

'Be my guest,' I said.

'I'll have another vodka Martini.'

'I didn't mean it like that.'

'Don't worry,' said Arlene. 'I didn't take it like that.'

Arlene stayed for an hour or two and drank three Martinis. Not wanting to monopolize her, I polished glasses after that first exchange and talked to the other customers. Arlene didn't talk to anyone. When she'd downed the third cocktail, she put her glass on the counter, swivelled on her stool, slid herself off it, and left without a look at anyone. I watched her go. She wasn't as tall as she'd seemed. The way she carried herself magicked a few inches on to her height. So did her stilettos. A breeze of perfume lingered behind her. I can smell it now, more than five months since she left. Perhaps I'm imagining it.

That was how Arlene introduced herself to me.

The trouble with talking about events in retrospect is that one knows what's to come. I can't tell you what happened a year ago without it being coloured by what's happened since. Even without what's happened since, Arlene's first appearance was an event.

I can't say that women never drink in here on their own, but it doesn't happen often. When Arlene came in for the first time, I expected it to be the last, whatever she said about hanging around. She wasn't meeting anyone. She wasn't local, so far as I knew. She would brighten one evening, then be gone. It was when she came back a second time, then a third, that I realized that Arlene was rewriting the rule book. By the fourth and fifth visits, it was clear that Arlene didn't possess a rule book, for this or for anything.

I can't deny I was soft on her. It wasn't just that she was good-looking, and sexy as hell. There was some other quality to Arlene that made me feel protective toward her. I don't think I was alone in that. I think every guy felt the same way. Arlene was someone who invited protection, then declined it when it was offered. Not that it was on offer from me. There are lines and barriers, and it's as well to respect them. Still, Marcie sensed my feelings that first night.

'How's your new girlfriend?' she asked, when we were in bed.

'You're not meant to know about her.'

'I had a little peek through the door when you were chatting her up.'

'She's hot,' I said.

'The type who likes men fifteen years older than herself, do you reckon?'

'Ten,' I said. 'It can't be more than ten.'

'At least fifteen, I'd say. More like twenty.'

'You're just saying that. Anyhow, think of all the young men who come in here. I'm allowed the one, aren't I?'

This is standard banter. Usually it's the other way about, and I tease her. It comes to the same thing. We allow each other our fantasies, such as they are, and don't feel threatened by them. Jealousy doesn't come into it. Besides, Arlene was no more likely to want me than the young men with big muscles and tight sweatshirts were likely to want Marcie. Our feet are on the ground. We know our market worth. Neither of us has grabbed a bargain, but we've each got good value.

Sometimes I forget how long I've been doing this job. That's assuming you can call it a job. It's more a way of life, a way of living in one building at split levels. One level is reserved for Marcie; the other for such of the world as passes our way, aka our customers. The levels overlap. At night, it's a bar where men come as a respite from home, or because they're lonely, or both. At lunchtime there's a different clientele. Then it's all sorts of people coming in from work for a light meal.

Marcie does lunchtimes. She does lunchtimes and I do evenings. That's the way it works. When we were younger, I did my shift solo. Marcie has always had help at midday, so she can stand behind the bar looking proprietorial. In the evenings, I do the same now. For the past five years, I've had Steve to help me out six nights a week. He does Sunday lunchtimes on his own, and sometimes Sunday evenings. We don't serve food then, and Marcie and I take the day off. He's a good kid, Steve. Marcie knows his family: they farm someplace close to where she comes from. I wanted to hire someone else at the time, but Marcie was insistent I should take the kid. I haven't regretted it. I don't know why we still call him the kid. He must be nearly thirty now, with two children of his own. He brings them to the bar sometimes and Marcie makes a real fuss of them. His wife's got a high-paid job, so Steve minds the children during the day and helps me in the evenings. He's as good-natured as you like, scratching his thick black hair in bemusement at our customers, smiling at the world in his lopsided way.

The building that houses the bar, and which is also where we live, is in fact two buildings. The bar is the taller part, the older part, and the part nearest the road. Rumour says that it was a farm building once, but rumour says so many things that it's impossible to say for certain. It has a pitched roof, and exposed beams, and gables at each end. Our living area was bolted on at a later point. It is square and functional, and of no interest. It has a flat roof, out of sight at the back, which we use as a sun terrace when there's any sun.

On this roof, there's a window in one of the gable ends of the bar area. Usually, it's covered with an old board, in case Marcie or I wander about in the nude without thinking. Not that we do, but just in case. Wouldn't want to excite the customers. When it's warm, I eat my lunch up there, while Marcie supervises the midday trade below. Sometimes I take down the board and observe the comings and goings. I have this curiosity about how we function. Why we function, come to that. What's the point of it? The gofer running from one table to another, putting down plates, picking up plates; Marcie standing behind the counter, taking money, giving money back.

It's like a nature programme on one of those channels that nobody watches, where zillions of ants go scurrying around the place as if their lives depended on it. Maybe they do depend on it. All that endeavour. All that ferrying about of leaves, and the nibbling of them, and beating off attacks from hostile ants, and the other stuff that goes with being an ant. What's the point of it? I mean, we need to eat, but why generally do we do it?

The best answer I can come up with is that it's to do with continuity. It's to do with prolonging the species into the future. It's to do with performing repetitive tasks for millions of years, so there's always a next generation to go on performing them. To what ultimate end, I've no idea. All I know is, when I think of purpose in these terms, I have to stop thinking. I have to pretend to myself that it's to do with shifting plates and glasses, and counting money. I don't want to think of the next generation anymore. We don't now, Marcie and me.

I tend to put customers into boxes. There are the regulars, the ones that turn up several times a week, the ones that think this entitles them to a piece of us: a time share in the real estate that is Marcie and me. There are the semi-regulars, the ones I see a few times each month, whose names I know, if I can remember them, whose stories I know, if I don't confuse them with some-one else's. Then there are the strangers, the ones who turn up once or twice and are gone in the wind. These are the evening customers I'm talking about. I expect much the same can be said of the lunchtime trade. I wouldn't know. You'd have to ask Marcie.

The ones who belong in a box are Marcie and me. We're the ones who live here, who work here, who spend our lives in the place. Others flow in and out, at times of their own choosing, with no respect for boxes and labels. The most loyal of them begin as strangers. You see them for the first time with no idea if you'll see them again. Later, when you feel you've known them your entire life, you forget that you once met them for the first time, and you forget what impression they made on you, or whether you liked them. You like them now, that's for sure, or at least you go out of your way to notice their good points. Of course you do. They give you money, so why wouldn't you be well disposed toward them? Doesn't mean you liked the look of them when they first walked in.

Once I kept a sign behind the bar that read 'NO POLITICS ALLOWED HERE'. That was after we'd had a couple of fights and the cops had to come and sort them out. Both fights made the front page of the local paper. For a while afterwards, people we'd never seen before came in and looked around, as if weighing up the prospect of another showdown. I didn't reckon on making my bar a haven for every screwball out there, so I put up the sign. Later, I took it down again. The place had gotten too quiet. We still talked, but about things we agreed on, which takes half the point out of talking. Human beings need to argue and, if you ask me, we need to argue more than we did before.

Nelson used to disagree with that proposition, which proves the point in my opinion. Nelson disagreed with every proposition. He would disagree with his own propositions if he heard them made by someone else. Nelson was our resident propagandist at the time. He was all right, but he did like an argument.

'People have always argued,' Nelson said. 'Why should you think they need to argue any more or any less than before?'

'Because everything's gotten the same,' I said. 'It's standardized. We're born the same, grow up the same, work the same, eat the same, live the same, die the same

same. Time was when we were individuals, when we knew what was different about us. Now, the only way we can assert ourselves is to tell other people they're wrong. It makes us feel there's a point to us.'

'Bullshit,' said Nelson. 'I tell other people they're wrong because they are wrong, not to make a point about myself. But what the hell do I know?'

That used to be one of Nelson's phrases. He said it to make the opposite point: that he knew everything about most things, and it was other people who didn't know what the hell they were talking about. He put it the other way round to make it sound better. Nelson is a failed politician, which he also put differently. A bull of a man, late forties I'd say, he runs a state-wide charity, based here in town. My personal theory is that, if you run a charity, you have to spend your days being nice to people, which must be tough for someone who prefers having arguments. I think the bar was Nelson's antidote to the day job. He's an OK guy, but not someone we'd have chosen as a friend if we got to choose. In the end, I did get to choose, which is one reason we don't see him any longer.

We don't have much time for friends, doing this. It's not that we don't have them. Having both grown up in the town, we've got plenty. But we don't get to see them much, unless they drink here, and the only one who does that reliably is Mike. I was in the same class as Mike at school. We've been friends since we were knee high. In practice, our friends are the regulars, which is a one-sided arrangement. They decide that they like our bar. They decide that they like us, or can tolerate us. They spend their money here when they feel like it, and expect us to talk to them in return. We don't have a say in the matter, assuming we want to build a clientele. They self-certify as our friends. Except that they wouldn't refer to us as their friends, most of them, because they have other lives, from which this is a diversion, and they have other friends. We don't have another life.

The worst of it is when you lose a regular, someone who's been coming in for years, most nights maybe, who suddenly stops coming. Sometimes they tell you the reason face to face: they're moving to another town, for example. Those ones come and say goodbye, visit again if they happen to be passing. Sometimes you don't know the reason at the time, but you find out later: they've split up with their wife, let's say. Other times, you don't know, and you never discover.

Jack Nightingale was a case in point. I hadn't thought of him in a while, until Arlene reminded me that first night she came in. Jack had been a good customer for ten years or more. I couldn't call him a regular, because his habits weren't regular. He'd come in most nights for a week or two, then we'd not see him for a couple of months. Jack lived in what I call the bastard town next door, for reasons I'll explain later if I remember, but he liked to drink in my bar. I expect it had to do with the women who sometimes accompanied him. Not to put too fine a point on it, they looked like tramps. You wouldn't want to be seen canoodling with women like that in your own home town, I imagine. Jack said he was divorced. Lots of people say that, and maybe they are and maybe they're not.

His line of business took him over five or six states. That's why we wouldn't see him for weeks at a time. So when he didn't show up for one week, two weeks, three weeks, it came as no surprise. He must have been gone more than a month before I noticed I hadn't seen him in a while. I haven't seen him since.

How old was Jack at that point? Getting on for seventy, I'd say. Still with the appearance of a '40s matinée idol, with a Clark Gable moustache that an amateur cartoonist might have drawn with a crayon. Still working; still looking trim; still with young women on his arm. They were probably paid for, but all the same. He could have married one of them and gone to live in Hawaii. I didn't know he was dead; I sort of presumed he was. The fact is you never know.

As I told Arlene, it had been a good five years since Jack Nightingale had last walked through these doors. Five years, would you believe it? No one else from the bastard town drinks here, and I don't see anyone who lives there, so I've never known what happened to him. And I wouldn't go looking. That would be against the rules, if there were any rules. Customers are entitled to their privacy. Even when they're dead. They're entitled to their privacy, and they're entitled to their secrets. They can invent a life story that's one hundred per cent organic bullshit, and I will be obliged to believe it, and to go on believing it for years.

I don't get the same privileges in return. Everyone knows the facts about me and Marcie, most of them, because there's no opportunity to disguise them, not that I'd want to. It sounds as if I'm bitching about my work, but I'm not. I enjoy it. I can't think of anything I'd have enjoyed more, apart from teaching. It's never dull. I don't know who's going to show up tomorrow, or who's never going to show up again. Maybe, one Halloween, an army of the missing will manifest themselves. A regular platoon of ex-regulars.

For a short while, too short a while, Arlene was one of the regulars. She belonged to an era. No, that's wrong. The era belonged to her. Along with Davy and Nelson and Mike, and Franky when he came back, and Steve behind the bar, and Marcie and me. That bunch of us. That was Arlene's era. We never did take a group photograph.

It started in February last year, as I said. That was when the nine months of Arlene began. The weather was mild, and we thought we'd escaped winter that year. We hadn't. Winter had gone on an extended vacation and didn't get back till March, full of energy, wanting to be everyone's best friend. Temperatures were below zero for much of that month and enough snow lay on the ground to make a statement. It deterred all but the most hardy. My regulars were among the most hardy, Arlene included. I was going to say it was during March that the rest of us got to know Arlene, but we never got to know her. She got to know us.

I assumed she was also getting to know the town, but I don't think she ever did. Later, after she'd gone, gone for the last time, I used to mention her to people in the stores and around the place, assuming they'd know who she was. Only a couple of people did. They were both called Jack, as it happens, so she must have been doing her homework. For the most part, when Arlene came to town, she came to the bar, and this was the only place she came. That was what I figured later. Now I think of it, she once called the town a dump, although she had the grace to apologize afterwards.

That's why I think she was a city girl. City people think that all small towns are dumps. City people thrive on artificial highs, legal or otherwise. They think that places where people sit around and talk to each other are boring. I appreciate that I'm biased. I was born and raised here, and I like it, and I haven't travelled much, and I can't compare it with anywhere else.

No, Arlene was a city girl. The question is whether that city was Pittsburgh or not.

This is not a big place: ten thousand people or so. You can get most everything you need here, so why trouble to go elsewhere? It's not me saying that: it's the general view of people around here. I asked Arlene what she'd got against the place. She said she'd got nothing against it; the place had something against her. It couldn't make space for a girl who'd seen the ocean. I told her people had seen the ocean on TV and that was good enough for them. Before TV, folk didn't have the means to travel. Since TV, they haven't had the need. Why go to the world when the world will come to you on a screen? Not my point of view exactly, but that's how people look at things here. Arlene didn't get it.

I think she came from another planet, and I'm close to meaning that literally. Some people do, or seem to. Some people's heads are in a place so different to everybody else's that they don't inhabit the same world. Everyone else in the bar, everyone else in my life, is more or less predictable. Once you've worked out their personalities, you know how they'll behave. They've been programmed on the production line. Unless some extreme event makes them go haywire, they'll be faithful to their factory settings till the day they die. I include myself in that description. Not Arlene.

By March, she was one of the boys. She drank and told stories like the rest of us. She'd been granted the accolade of her own seat at the bar. Most of the counter is long and straight, but at one end it goes bulbous and there's a group of high stools around that end, where the regulars sit. Sometimes they're at tables with each other, or with other people, but when they're at the bar, that's where they sit. Sometime in March, Arlene got her own stool, in the middle of the group, and from then to November only one other person sat on it. No one has sat on it since, as a matter of fact. At least, not that I've seen.

What separated Arlene from the boys, apart from the obvious, was that she never talked about herself. After four or five visits, we were none the wiser. For one thing, it was hard to say how much money she had. First glance, at her clothes, at her car, at her demeanour, said it must be a lot. First impressions can mislead. As Marcie pointed out, thrift shops sell designer clothes. The shiny black sports car was showy, but it came from one of the cheaper ranges and could have been second-hand. A detailed inventory of her belongings might not have produced a large tally.

Mike is our go-to guy where money is concerned. He came top of the class in math when we were kids, so I wasn't surprised that he got a job as a bank teller. Thirty-five years on, he's still a bank teller, so perhaps math is all he can do. Marcie and I feel protective toward him and encourage him to say more than he does. I asked him how rich he thought Arlene was.

'Whatever she's got,' said Mike, 'it's not what it looks like she's got.'

We were impressed with this pronouncement until we realized we didn't have the first idea what Mike meant. We asked him to be less obscure.

'What I mean,' said Mike, 'is that Arlene is someone who presents as being comfortably off – not rich, not poor – and I'd say that's the one thing she's not. I reckon that maybe she's loaded and what we're seeing is the tip of an iceberg. Or she's skint and it's all done with loans and mirrors. Don't ask me which.'

'Which?' I asked.

'If I had to guess, I'd say skint. I'm still waiting for her to buy me a drink.'

Then there was the fact that no one knew where Arlene lived. She didn't tell that either, except it was somewhere out in the boondocks, which may or may not have been true. About two nights a week, she'd come to the bar. It varied. Sometimes it was most nights; sometimes we didn't see her for a couple of weeks. She'd slip into the parking lot and leave her car neatly by the door. Then, a little before closing time, she'd smile her goodbyes and slip out again.

She didn't live in town. I suppose I can't be sure about that either. Let's just say that, if she did live in town, she can't have left the house much. None of us saw her there, not in the stores, not out on the street, not anywhere. Nor did we see her car. And it's not a large town.

One night, Nelson thought he'd follow her and see where she went. When he came in the next evening, we clustered round to hear the news. There was no news.

'Trailed her to the Interstate,' said Nelson. 'Then she took off like a rocket. Don't know where she went.'

'Which direction?'

'West.'

'Did she know you were following her?'

'I don't think so,' said Nelson.

'She must have done. Wouldn't have taken off like that otherwise.'

'Maybe she always drives like that.'

''Bout time you got a faster car, Nelson.'

''Bout time I stopped chasing shadows,' said Nelson.

A couple of other guys tried the same thing in the weeks that followed, guys with faster cars. Didn't do them any good. Arlene drove a couple of miles down the road, pulled off at a truck stop and waited till they got bored. For all we knew, she could have been living in a trailer park. That wouldn't surprise me in the slightest.

So many things about Arlene we never knew. I can tell you one thing we did know, though.

In the corner of the bar stands a jukebox. Goodness knows how old it is. If you press the first button, you can probably hear Moses read the Ten Commandments. I inherited it when I bought the place. I've lost count of the number of people who've made me offers for it, but I'm not selling. A bar needs a jukebox.

It has always played the same records. The fifty discs on it when I took the place over are still on it. I know that jukeboxes are supposed to be up to date. But the customers seem to like it the way it is and, if they don't, Marcie and I do.

I was at the counter one evening, in the usual way. I was aware that a song was playing in the background. I couldn't have told you what it was but for what happened next. Arlene jumped off her stool and rushed up to me in a state of agitation. That was two surprises in one. Arlene didn't rush and she didn't get agitated.

'How do you turn the music off?' she asked.

'You don't.'

'You have to. I can't listen to this.'

'It's only a song, Arlene.'

'I can't listen to it. Please turn it off.'

I walked over to the machine and turned it off. Then I turned it back on, put in another coin, put on another record. A song that Arlene liked.

The song she couldn't abide was 'My Guy' by Mary Wells. I don't know why. I asked her and she wouldn't tell me. It wasn't that she disliked the song, she said, it was just that, just that . . . Silence. Something must have happened to Arlene that made her unable to listen to it. Now, whenever I hear 'My Guy' playing, I think of her. The song she refused to hear has become her signature tune.

2

Holy Moses, it was cold that March. Truly cold. Snow blanketed the fields for weeks. High winds built ridges along the ditches. Gritters kept the roads going, but the traffic flowed slowly, like blood trickling through the arteries of the aged. We kept warm, and I searched for signs of spring.

'Don't look too hard,' said Marcie. 'Cows will be in their barns a while yet.'

Marcie comes from a farming family, as you might guess. They've got a few hundred acres, ten miles west of here, next to the farm where Steve was raised, as it happens. Her dad died some years ago, her mom more recently, and Marcie's two brothers run the place now. Sometimes we go over on a Sunday lunchtime, while Steve minds the shop. Marcie thinks of the farm as home. A patch of land does that for you. I don't think of the house where I grew up as home. I don't think of it much at all.

She was nineteen when we started dating and I was twenty-one. She wasn't a great looker, and neither was I.

Marcie's on the short side, trim, with mid-brown curly hair. Smart with it. And she's got a great personality, as long as you don't get on the wrong side of it. I've taken care not to do that. People said we made a good team, the way they do when they can't think of anything better to say. It was true, though, and it still is, and although I once hoped for a more dynamic phrase to define us, I settle for that one now. We'd known each other for a while because we went to the same school. We were in different years, but it was almost like we sized each other up then and filed the conclusions away for future reference. By the time we started dating, we'd made up our minds about each other a long time before.

I won't talk about children. I'll just say that we had twins, a son and a daughter, and now we don't. It has brought us closer. At least, I think it has; maybe I'm deluding myself. At the same time, it has made us more distant from other members of our families. I have relatives, somewhere, some of them in this town in fact, but I seldom see them, and it's the same with Marcie, apart from her two brothers. We see more of those two these days, now their children have grown up. We didn't see so much of them when their kids were at the farm.

Marcie was a shop girl when we married. She worked at the haberdasher's on Main Street. It's not there now. I was training to be a teacher, something I did for twelve years or more. It wasn't a coincidence we both did jobs that involved talking to people. It's what we like doing.

I thought I'd be a teacher for the rest of my life, but things happened, life changed, and I stopped wanting to be with kids every day. Fifteen years ago, with some money from my parents, and some from Marcie's, and some savings, we got this place and here we are.

It was in those weeks before the snows melted that Arlene began to talk more freely. Most nights she sat on her stool like the proverbial mouse, silent, whiskers twitching at what others were saying. Then, from time to time, she'd decide to hold court.

'When I was growing up,' she said on one occasion; 'when I was, I don't know, maybe fourteen or fifteen, I used to watch the man across the street in his room. We lived on the fourth floor, and so did he, and the street was quite narrow, so he wasn't far away. He didn't have curtains. When it was dark and he had the light on, I could see him clearly. He couldn't see me, though. I didn't want him prying on me. I'd draw my curtains, and turn the light off, and pull a chair up to the window. Then I'd peep through the curtains and watch him. I'd do it for hours on end sometimes.

'I called him John, like he was John Doe. He became a friend of mine. I never met him. You'd think that, living so close, we'd be bound to meet in the street, or in the corner store, but we never did. I kind of liked that. He could stay the person I wanted him to be. If I'd met him, there would have been something that wasn't what I expected, or what I wanted. I don't know what he did in the daytime. He could have been at work, I guess. I was at school most of the time, and besides, it was one of my rules not to look in the daytime. He was my stranger in the night, except that by the end he no longer seemed like a stranger. He seemed like an old friend.'

'Did you see him naked?' The question came from Marcie. I had toyed with asking it, and hadn't dared. If that question had come from a man, it would have taken the conversation somewhere else. Coming from a woman, it sounded almost innocent.

'Oh, no,' said Arlene. 'Certainly not.' She seemed shocked at the suggestion. It wasn't the only time it occurred to me that, while Arlene might look tarty, underneath she was prim as hell.

'There was nothing like that,' she said. 'He must have had a bedroom at the back. At least I imagine he did, because at eleven every night he turned out the light and he was fully clothed when he did it. That was the death moment, what I called the death moment. There was a split second before the room went dark when his silhouette was framed in the halo of the dimming light. I thought that dying must be like that, except that death doesn't happen every night. Or perhaps it does.'

'What did he do all evening?' I don't know why I asked. I wasn't interested in what he did. Why would I be? I suppose I was interested in what Arlene had done, and why she did it.

'Not much. Sometimes he'd watch TV and I'd see the

25

blue light of the screen flickering. Sometimes he'd read a book, or a newspaper. Other times he sat there. I suppose he didn't do anything. It was a life stripped down to the essentials, just John and his room, and a few items of furniture, and what was in his head.'

'Poor guy,' I said.

'Why? Perhaps he liked to live that way. I don't know that he was unhappy. It could have been his choice. He might have said to himself at some point that life was too complicated, and it was best to stick to the basics. I admit it was sad, though. Did he fear being overwhelmed, do you think? Or was it a sense of inadequacy? Did he think he had nothing to say, and that no one would be interested in him? Or didn't he know how to do it? Had no one taught him how you go up to a stranger and talk to them? I don't know. What seems simple often isn't simple at all. I'm not sure what's natural in people. It varies, I think. My natural state is to be alone, and then force myself to make the effort of being sociable.'

'Or,' said Marcie, 'your natural state is to be sociable, but you like to think of yourself as someone who's alone.'

'Who knows?' said Arlene. 'I suppose the issue is whether you're frightened of being alone. Completely alone. I don't think I am frightened of that, not anymore. I think you can teach yourself not to be frightened of it. Maybe that's what John learned to do, and I wanted to copy it by watching him. In summer, he'd raise the window and lean half out of it, smoking a cigarette and drinking a can of beer, staring out at the street. I used to imagine what he was thinking.'

'He could have been thinking of you. Staring at your window,' I said.

'Oh, no,' said Arlene. 'No, I don't think so. He was looking down at the sidewalk, I'd say. It was funny. His cigarettes lasted six and a half minutes. I used to smoke myself. My cigarettes lasted different amounts of time. His lasted six and a half minutes. Every time.'

'You counted?'

'Yes,' said Arlene. 'I kept a notebook. I wrote down everything he did and the time he did it. I knew more about him than he knew about himself.'

Marcie raised one eyebrow at me. That's one of her tricks. Sometimes I try to do it back, but I can't.

'How old was he?' I asked.

'Fifty, maybe. He didn't seem to have any friends. No one came to his apartment and he never went out, or not in the evenings. Imagine spending every night of the year in a small room on your own. Life is sad. No point pretending it's not. I already knew life was sad. Once I had thought it was sad only when you were a child. When I looked at John, I could see that the sadness never ended. I knew he was my future. I looked at him and thought that was how I would be when I grew up.'

'It isn't, though, is it?' said Marcie. 'You don't spend every night on your own.' Arlene didn't respond to that.

'What about your family?' I asked. 'Where were they while you were looking out of your window?'

'Out,' said Arlene. 'My mom worked evenings.'

'And your dad?'

'Never been quite sure about him. He wasn't at home, anyway.'

'Your mom wasn't married?'

'No. Never.'

'Did you have brothers and sisters?'

'No idea. Not living with us, anyhow. Maybe half-brothers or half-sisters, somewhere. I don't know.'

'So it was just you and your mom at home,' said Marcie.

'Yes,' said Arlene. 'But it wasn't really a home. It was three rooms with two people. One of them happened to have given birth to the other.'

'Is your mom alive?'

'No. Not anymore. Sad.'

'Doesn't do any good to talk that way,' said Marcie. 'Life's not sad unless you make it sad. And it's not happy unless you make it happy. It's not what it is; it's what you make it.'

This is one of Marcie's firmest beliefs. I've heard it stated a hundred times. It's the closest she comes to sounding unsympathetic. Other than to people she doesn't like. I told her that once. Marcie's view is that, while everyone deserves sympathy, it's not always what they need. She can be surprisingly dogmatic for someone whose nature is not to be dogmatic.

'You're wrong,' said Arlene, definitively.

That was the closest I heard Arlene come to being sure of anything. It was also the end of the conversation; it had nowhere to go after that. The image has stayed with me, though, of Arlene spending her teenage years peeping out at the world through closed curtains.

Hovering around this and every conversation with her was the vague presence of Jack. However little we knew, what we thought we knew was that she was looking for Jack. Now I consider the matter, it seems appropriate that the most concrete thing about Arlene concerned someone with a nebulous existence. At one time or another, most of us tried to discover who Jack was. That night, it was Mike who had a go.

'Who's Jack?' he asked. Mike's like me. He goes direct, when he goes at all. Like me, I expect he was wondering if this guy across the street was Jack. John Doe. Jack Doe. Could've been.

'I'll tell you when I find out,' said Arlene.

'When's that likely to be?'

'No time soon, at the present rate of progress.'

'I mean, was he your husband? Your lover?'

'Oh, no, nothing like that,' said Arlene.

'Why are you looking for him?'

'Because I need to find him. He's important. Or was important. At least, I believe so.'

'You think he's in town?'

'I don't know,' said Arlene. 'He used to be in town.

And in other places too. I don't know where he is now. He could be anywhere. Or nowhere.'

'But you think he might be in town?'

'Stop pumping me, will you?' said Arlene. 'I'll tell you when I'm good and ready. If I ever am. And if I feel like it.'

Mike looked hard at her. 'You're some weird lady,' he said.

'What makes you say that?'

He shrugged his shoulders. 'Well, you are, aren't you? Weird.'

'And you're not?'

'I wouldn't say so. Hey. Steve. Would you say I was weird?'

'Weird as hell,' said Steve.

'There you are, then,' said Arlene. 'I guess we're both weird.'

I listened to this from a few feet away. I admired Mike for the attempt. We all wanted to know the answer.

Despite it having seemed a harmless conversation, it affected Arlene deeply. She got up from her stool, and went to sit on another stool, apart from us. There was a theatricality to her movement, but no petulance. She sat there, looking a little the other way, that's to say between full face and profile, with every known misery in her expression. As we half watched her, pretending not to, we waited for the tears to fall.

They didn't, to begin with. They lay dammed behind

large, flat, dark eyes, no escape route open. Tear ducts seemed blocked as autumn streams, debris lining their beds, the dryness of summer months breaking the habits of moisture. Then, after several minutes, the pressure became irresistible and the waters found weak points in the mortar and crumbled her defences.

If I were a religious man, I could say they were tears of pity for the world, the tears of a Madonna. I am not a religious man, or not in that way. We aren't, around here; not in that way. We know what life is like and we don't cry about it. We were taught self-sufficiency by our ancestors, who learned it from experience. We have broad shoulders, but not broad enough to carry the world. Our own problems are a sufficient burden. We take the hand we're dealt, uncomplaining, and expect others to do the same. Perhaps we lack sympathy. Like Marcie, I think I'd say that sympathy has its limits. After that you have to get on with stuff.

'You all right, Arlene?' asked Davy, eventually.

Arlene looked at him in a considered way. She got up and came to sit on her own stool again. 'Yeah, I'm OK,' she said. 'I guess.'

We were all guessing, it would appear.

At some point, someone was going to make a pass at Arlene. Everyone knew it, including Arlene, I imagine. The question was who and when. Of course, it might have happened already, without me knowing. But Marcie would have sensed it, you can be sure of that. It's safe to

31

say that by mid-March it hadn't happened. Amongst the regulars, there were two contenders, Davy and Nelson.

I don't know what it is with guys. Maybe I was the same when I was younger. I'm sure I was. In the days of Arlene's early visits, those two were convinced that she came to the bar to see them. They both told me that. I don't think Arlene was interested in either of them. Even though she ended up with Davy, I don't think she had more than a passing fondness for him. I believe she was doing what she said she was doing: looking for Jack. But that couldn't have occupied all her time. Who knows what she did with the rest of it, when she wasn't in the bar? I can't offer a comment on that. But I think she was bored, and I think she was lonely, and I think that Davy helped to pass the time while she was searching. Anyway, that's conjecture now. At that moment, Davy and Nelson were vying for Arlene's attention, and I would have said that Davy was ahead by a length or two. It was surely no coincidence that, on an evening when he was absent, Nelson decided to stake his claim before he found that the gold was already mined.

Nelson was in an expansive mood that night, buying drinks for all and sundry, for once appearing to talk about something other than himself. Technically speaking, he might not have been buying the drinks. When he first started coming here, Nelson asked for the till receipts, to the point where I handed them over without him needing to make the request. He was not alone in that but, since his job is running a charity, I took a suspicious view of it. Technically speaking, it might have been the donors to Nelson's charity who were footing the bill that night. Failing that, it might have been us taxpayers. Whoever it was, we got free drinks.

'I'm coming under a lot of pressure at the moment,' he said, once he'd got tired of not talking about himself.

This was one of Nelson's many irritating habits. He made these enigmatic statements that obliged you to seek clarification, which made it sound as though you were interested in the answer, which then gave him permission to talk about himself for the next hour. Steve was better at playing the patsy for Nelson than I was.

'Why's that?' he asked.

'They want me to run again.'

'For Congress?'

'That's right.'

'Who's "they"?' asked Arlene. Oh, no, Arlene. That's what he wants you to ask. I should have warned you. Don't listen to a word he says. It's bullshit.

'I shouldn't really say,' said Nelson. 'The party bosses. I can't be more specific than that.' He looked at Arlene, anticipating the next question.

'Politics sucks,' said Arlene. Yes, Arlene. That's my girl. I've said that to Nelson a thousand times. It sounds so much better when you say it.

Nelson laughed in a way that suggested he thought Arlene was joking. That was because he did think Arlene was joking. For one thing, he thought that no one could seriously believe that politics sucked. For another, since Arlene had come to the bar because she was infatuated with him, obviously she wouldn't be dismissive of a subject so dear to his heart. Nelson concluded that Arlene must want to hear more of politics, and of his own political achievements. So he began to answer the questions he had prompted Arlene to ask, and which she hadn't. This could have continued for the rest of the evening but, after a few minutes, Arlene set down her unfinished glass, smiled sweetly, said, 'See you, guys,' and headed for the door.

Nelson laughed again. 'I like a woman who plays hard to get,' he said.

'Nelson,' I said. 'Arlene isn't playing hard to get. She is hard to get. For you, she's impossible to get.'

'For anyone, I'd have thought,' said Marcie. She put her hands on her hips for emphasis, the way that Ollie Hardy did. That's another of her mannerisms. She's always doing that.

'Bullshit,' said Nelson. 'I'll show you.' He strode out through the doors.

We didn't see them again that night. When Nelson next came in, he had a scratch down his face. Davy, who didn't know the story, asked him the cause of it. Nelson didn't answer directly, but gave the impression it was the result of a night of wild lovemaking. The fact that he winked at Steve and me was meant to implicate Arlene.

When Arlene came in herself a little while later, she ignored Nelson. On reflection, that was the night that she started to take an interest in Davy. On further reflection, it was Arlene who made the first move, not that Davy was raising objections. By the end of March, they were an item.

It's strange this business of who ends up with who, and how. Admittedly, Arlene didn't end up with Davy long term but, if she had, it could have been partly because of what Nelson did or said in the parking lot. When I first started dating Marcie, it had to do with what had happened to her with someone else, not that I knew that at the time. It's timing and coincidence, that's all. Collisions and near misses. Nothing else.

I've not said much about Davy till now. The first time he came into the bar, he was unconscious. I've known customers who arrived vertical and left horizontal. This was the only time it happened the other way around. What occurred, I discovered later, was that there were these four guys, Davy being one of them, having a debate on a street corner in town. They decided to adjourn the argument to a bar. One of the four occasionally drank here, so this is where they came, in the same car. During the journey, the argument became more heated, so that when they spilled out into my parking lot, a fight commenced. We heard the noise from the bar, stepped outside as quick as we could, and got ourselves ringside seats for the bout. It didn't last long. Davy got knocked cold. The others decided enough was enough, picked him up, carried him into the bar and laid him on a table.

Marcie got the first-aid box and I went to call the cops. The other three were anxious I shouldn't do that and began fiddling in their pockets for twenty-dollar bills. The more bills got produced, the more I could see their point. Then Davy came round, sat up on the table, realized what was happening, and added his vote to the no-cops lobby. Marcie patched him up and gave him a brandy. Two of the protagonists disappeared in the car, and I called a cab to take Davy and the fourth guy away. We gossiped about it the next few nights and thought that was the end of it.

A week or so later, Davy showed up again on his own, face still the worse for wear, holding a bunch of cheap flowers as a thank-you gift for Marcie. That was a courteous gesture, so I stood him a beer and he ended up staying the rest of the evening. By the end of the month, Davy was a regular. That was two years ago.

To start with, he said nothing about himself, except that he'd recently come to live and work in town, but wasn't from these parts. We knew that already. After a while, he was forced to tell us more. Forced by peer pressure, I mean. The fact is that you can hold back for a few evenings. You can't do it for ever. Being a regular in a bar is like joining a poker syndicate: there's a stake to get you into the game. Once you've laid it down, you don't have to raise it, and you don't have to meet another guy's raise, but the opening stake has to be sitting there on the table. Davy sussed that after a while. Perhaps he'd never been a regular in a bar before. Or in a poker school.

None of us believed the story Davy told, or not all of it. He must have been early forties when he made his debut with us. He was tall, good-looking and alert. Sandy hair, thinning. He looked like a regular guy, the sort you'd expect to be married with a kid or two. On the waiting list at the country club, that sort of thing. He seemed bright enough. Marcie and I guessed he had some middle-ranking executive position. Davy didn't confirm these assumptions. What he did confirm was the one thing we already knew: he had a temper. It was Nelson who first got under Davy's skin when he tried to tease some information from him. This was ironic, because there was plenty we didn't know about Nelson, or weren't sure of.

'Your wife work?' he asked one evening.

'I don't have a wife,' said Davy.

'Split up, huh?'

'Never married,' said Davy. 'Not that it's any of your business.'

Nelson stared at the band of pale skin on Davy's wedding finger. 'Amazing what birthmarks people are born with,' he said.

That set Davy off. We learned in time that sarcasm and Davy didn't rub along too well, specially when the sarcasm was at his expense. His face reddened. He got up from his stool, knocking it over, and moved to grab

37

Nelson by the lapels. Nelson handled things well. He didn't react, just sat there unruffled. Big guys can afford to do that. Davy, realizing that it took two to have a fight and only one contestant had signed the contract, extricated himself from the situation, righted his stool and sat on it again.

'We don't have fights in here,' I said. 'Ever. I'm not counting the first time, because that was outside. Your first fight in here is your last. Is that clear, Davy?'

'Sure thing,' said Davy. 'I'm sorry, guys. I'm a little over-sensitive right now.'

The trouble with this exchange was that it shut the door on the substantive issues. We couldn't easily raise the subject again. We didn't believe he'd never been married. We didn't believe that the photo in his wallet was of his niece and nephew. The others thought the kids both looked like Davy. I didn't like to look at the picture myself. We played along with the fictions because, short of telling Davy he was a liar, there was no choice.

The question of his employment was resolved more easily. He said he worked as a pump attendant on the other side of town. We didn't believe that either, until Mike found him at the gas station one day. The job surprised Marcie and me. We thought he'd have something better than that. Davy must have felt the same way. He did it for a few months, then found another position. So it went on: a new job every few months, each one a little better than the last.

I don't know how much of Davy's affair with Arlene took place away from the bar, but plenty took place within it. For a while, Arlene was in three or four nights a week, and Davy was in every night, waiting to see if Arlene would show. He never seemed to know if she would or not. They didn't appear to make prior arrangements. The nights that Arlene came, the two of them would sit together in a far corner, in rapt attention, wrapped up in each other. Sometimes, when they had sunk a few drinks, they would sing songs together, quietly, almost under their breath. Old songs, songs that must have meant something to them once, when they were young, when the world had seemed kinder. Not 'My Guy', obviously. They could pass an evening doing that. The first few times, people looked at them, surprised at the performance, or straining to catch the melody. After a while, no one paid them any mind.

I asked Davy why they did it. 'Better than talking,' he said. At the time, I thought he meant he didn't like talking to Arlene, or they didn't have much to say to each other. I don't think that was true. Other nights, they talked the whole time. I think he meant his reply literally: that they liked the talking, but liked the singing better. Perhaps they found they could sing things to each other that they could not say. Perhaps the melodies took them to happier corners of respective memories and let them linger there for the evening.

Before Arlene, Davy was one of the guys, one of the

regulars who would sit at his place at the bar, chewing the fat with the rest of us. After Arlene, Davy was a man apart: he was the one who talked to Arlene, and the two of them sat at their own table. We didn't talk to her so much, after that. There were two vacant stools at the regulars' end of the bar: Davy had removed himself from the group. There was no difficulty that I noticed. Everyone greeted him in the old way, and he them. But it was different.

When the snows melted in early April and spring came, what we hoped would be the spring, it was Marcie who suggested we should take a short break. We don't take vacations together as a rule. No reason why not. There are others we can trust to run the place. But we couldn't afford to do it when we started, and now we've gotten into the habit. Marcie goes to Colorado once a year, on her own. In the middle of August. On the anniversary. She's done it for each of the past fifteen years. I know she'd like me to go too. I don't feel I can face it. I go fishing sometimes, maybe a couple of times a year. But one of us stays behind. Vacations, proper vacations together, will need to wait for retirement.

Usually, on the nights when Arlene didn't turn up, Davy stayed as long as it took to establish that she wasn't coming and not much longer. During that time, he sat on his old stool at the bar, talking to me and whoever else was around. One night, Marcie and I were both there, and Marcie was agitating for her weekend break.

'Go to Coney Island,' said Davy.

'Why should we want to do that?' I said. 'It's a dump these days.'

We had an animated discussion about whether Coney Island was now officially a dump or not. The majority opinion was that, even if it was a dump, it was still Coney Island. I found it hard to dispute this view. I wasn't keen on going, but Davy was a strong advocate and Marcie became seized with the idea. The clincher came a few days later, when Davy announced that he and Arlene wanted to come too. Personally, I could resist the temptation of Coney Island, but I couldn't resist the temptation of a few solid days attempting to decipher the enigma that was Arlene. I also wanted to know about Jack. However little she knew about him, she knew more than she'd told us and I wanted to find out what it was.

The outing was arranged for a weekend in late April. We figured that Steve could cope with a weekend in the bar on his own, if a friend helped him on the Friday and Saturday nights. Marcie clucked around him like a mother hen, the way she always does with him, to make sure he knew what he needed to do. Marcie's two part-timers could manage the lunches between them. Everything was fixed, until I got cold feet about the jaunt. But Marcie was not to be denied her holiday.

'I'm going come hell or high water,' she said.

It rained for the next three weeks. The parking lot was a lake when we left.

3

A couple of hundred yards from the bar, going out of town, is a crossroads. There used to be a bench there, with a metal plaque to say it was in honour of E. A. Stuart. I don't know who E. A. Stuart was. I asked around town years ago, and no one knew. He must have been pretty old, because the bench was old, and I suppose they put it there when he died. They must have done unless they were psychic, because the plaque gave the year of his death.

When I was a kid, I used to sit on that bench, for hours on end sometimes. I watched the cars and trucks go by and wondered where they were headed. Perhaps E. A. Stuart did the same, watching the early Fords go by and wondering what the country was coming to if a horse and cart weren't good enough for a man.

Three of the roads led elsewhere: to some places I barely knew at the time, and to others I didn't know at all. I must have wondered about those places, what they were like, who lived there, whether I would go there someday. I must have done. But I don't remember that.

What I remember was watching the cars go the fourth way, back into town. There is Dr Bruce, returning from a call to someone sick. Oh, and there is Mrs Keeley, who lives near us and teaches at the school. These people were real to me, not the ones who went straight across the junction, from here to there, wherever those places were, but places I didn't know, and people I didn't know either.

I liked real people, familiar people. Mentally, I fitted them into their homes and workplaces as if I was tidying toys into the cupboard. I checked them out and I checked them in, making sure all was safe, all was well, that everyone was where they were meant to be. Maybe that's why I got this particular bar. A town-centre bar would have made more sense, money wise. I wanted this one, down from the crossroads. When business is slow, I wander up to the corner and check the comings and goings like I did when I was a kid.

The day before the expedition to Coney Island, I was standing on that corner, and I saw Franky Albertino drive by. At least, I thought it was Franky. He was driving fast and I didn't lock on to him till he was nearly gone, so I couldn't be sure. But people have an essence, something that is uniquely theirs. It's not a physical thing, or not only a physical thing. It's the way the figure's set, the way the face is set. It's an attitude thing. Anyone can mistake the looks of another person, especially if they don't know them well or haven't seen them in a while. I don't think I've ever mistaken a person when I've sensed their essence. That's how I knew it was Franky.

Franky was a good friend of mine when we were young. He had charm, bags of it, and at that age I thought charm was the best thing you could have, especially as I didn't have much of it myself. It was later that I came to see it as a mixed blessing. Sure, it can often get you what you want, but what you want may not be what you need. As kids, none of us knew that. Franky got his own way too easily, for his own good or for anyone else's. He was a leader and I was prepared to be led.

Girls came to be his main problem. Not that Franky would have seen it that way then, and maybe still wouldn't. Any more than the girls themselves did for a while. They weren't old enough to see beyond the charm. In those days, they prostrated themselves before him like the acolytes of a religious cult before their guru. One girl who didn't do that was Marcie. That's possibly why I came to respect Marcie, and to trust her judgement. And, of course, to marry her, although that came a while later.

Franky was flavour of the month for nearly five years, which was a pretty good run, you have to admit. Then he went the way of all flavours, except perhaps chocolate. It wasn't simply that he fell out of fashion. There were more concrete reasons. Rumour had it that he'd got a girl pregnant. He borrowed money too. Not much, it must be said, but from lots of people, me among them, so it mounted up. He took care to repay some of it, which encouraged further loans. He never repaid all of it.

Then he left town. People like Franky always leave town in the end. Charm wears off, or at any rate becomes insufficient to sustain a career. There came to be too many people who remembered things that Franky had done, and wished he hadn't. You couldn't say the town had become too hot to hold him. That would be an exaggeration. Let's say there came to be a mutual, unspoken agreement between Franky and the people who had known Franky that it would be a good idea if he found some other place to practise his charm. In the olden times, it was the snake-oil salesmen and the preachers who moved on. These days, it's the Frankys of this world, and there's not a deal of difference. They're all peddlers of some kind of faith, and they all disappoint.

Franky must have left about thirty years earlier, and no one had seen hide nor hair of him since. He wasn't forgotten. People like Franky don't get forgotten. Sometimes we'd hear rumours of where he was, and what he was doing, and it was always something out of the ordinary, that made you think, 'Wow, I wish I was doing that.' There's no point saying what those things were because I've no reason to believe they were true. That's the other thing about people like Franky: they attract rumours. It's irrelevant whether the rumours are true, and mostly they're not.

As time went by, Franky was spoken of less frequently,

but with greater fondness. The pain he had caused began to be forgotten or overlooked. His behaviour came to be regarded as youthful high spirits, nothing more. What was remembered was that he'd been a character. Characters were two a dime when we were young. Now they're at a premium. It was with some excitement that I thought I saw him driving into town.

I told Marcie and she wasn't impressed.

'Wonder what he wants,' was all she said. I expect we'd have discussed it more, but we were busy packing for our trip to Coney Island, making sure everything was organized in the bar, and we got distracted.

It was a Friday morning when we set off. A pale sun inched its way over the horizon, catching drops of dew on the long grass, dancing a spectrum of colours down the wayside. In the fields, stalks of green barley waved at us, like the President does. Davy took the wheel and I sat beside him, looking out the window. I drive around town, but prefer not to drive too much on the open road these days. The women were in the back seat, asleep.

We were sitting there, four good people in a good old Ford, heading off to Coney Island. I shouldn't say we were good people, because perhaps we weren't. Maybe we were four middling people in a middling old Ford. There was a bartender and his wife, at least half their days behind them, unless there's a major advance in cryogenics. Not much to look forward to except more of the same, and then gradual decrepitude and death.

Remarkable how cheerful we keep in the circumstances. There were our two good friends, Davy and Arlene, except they weren't especially good friends, more random people we'd happened to have encountered in life and liked well enough to take this trip with.

Davy swerved to avoid a couple of cyclists, then jerked the sunshield down with his right hand. I looked the other way.

'Darned sun,' he said; 'can't see where the hell I'm going.'

We made our approach to Coney Island via Staten Island and the Brooklyn Bridge. I saw skyscrapers in the distance and wondered what planet they came from. Not my planet anyway. I had wanted to go to Manhattan over the weekend. It seemed a waste to come all this way and not see the city. But Davy said we didn't have the time, and Marcie said we didn't have the money, and Arlene didn't want to go anyplace except Coney Island, so I shut up.

Marcie was the only one of us who had been there before, so she was appointed tour guide. A visit made forty years or so earlier was not much preparation for the role. The place had slid downhill since then. Not literally, or it would have disappeared into the sea. Metaphorically. On second thoughts, perhaps I do mean literally.

We stayed at the Coney Island Hotel, where Marcie had stayed before. We arrived in the dark, which was the best time to see the place. Through flimsy curtains, a red-and-green neon sign jittered against the sky, flashing sporadic wattage into the room in which we half slept. Sometimes it was a red light, sometimes a green light, sometimes no light at all. 'CONEY IS AN H EL', it spelled to the world. The place was so broken, it couldn't get its own name right anymore. Or, again, maybe it did.

We'd agreed to meet the others in the breakfast room at eight. Arlene and Davy were already sitting there, looking more like a long-married couple than two people who'd got the hots for each other, which wasn't a good omen. We fetched our breakfasts from the buffet and sat on white plastic chairs, facing each other across a white plastic table. None of us said anything for a while.

'Tacky or what?' said Davy.

'I like tacky,' said Arlene. 'Every once in a while.'

'Tacky doesn't last,' said Davy.

'I don't expect any of it will last much longer,' I said. 'You don't get the impression this place is doing good business.'

'It's out of season,' said Marcie.

'How do you tell the difference?' asked Davy.

'Another twenty years and the whole lot will be gone,' I said.

'So will we,' said Arlene.

'I hope not,' I said. 'I'm planning on being around. You're not, Arlene?' Arlene said nothing.

After that, we decided to cheer up. It was a crap hotel in a crap location and outside it was pouring with rain but, hey, it was a vacation. Unappetizing though it was, it was something other than the daily grind.

'What plans has the tour guide made for us?' asked Davy.

'The tour guide hasn't made any definite plans,' said Marcie. 'The tour guide has more sense than to waste time making plans that everyone will want to change. However, we could go look at the amusement park . . .'

'. . . what's left of the amusement park,' said Davy, who'd been doing his homework.

'And go on some of the rides . . .'

'. . . if they're still open.'

'And take a stroll down the boardwalk, and have a dog at Nathan's. We should do that, if nothing else.'

'Sounds like a plan,' I said. 'Why don't we hit the boardwalk?'

When we got outside and saw the relentless wind and rain, we decided to postpone our visit to the boardwalk. Instead, we explored the hinterland of Coney Island. We paced Brighton Avenue, where delicatessens, law offices, tattoo parlours, groceries, dime stores, pawnbrokers, nail salons, loan shops, second-hand furniture emporia and fast-food outlets jostled cheek by jowl. The street itself lay under the blanket of the elevated subway tracks, the F-trains rumbling overhead through the morning. Although it was at ground level, it felt like a subterranean world where every known form of commercial enterprise competed for the same dollar.

When the weather eased, when we mistakenly thought it had eased, we emerged from this warren into the daylight of Surf Avenue. Sun pierced cloud fleetingly, brilliantly, and was then occluded. The rain began to fall again. Not heavy nor light, but in a steady, determined fall that looked as if it was settled in for centuries. Most people abandoned the sidewalk for shelter. We kept going, beneath umbrellas. This was a unanimous decision, taken without a vote.

'I like it when it rains,' said Arlene.

'Of course you do,' said Davy. 'You like everything that's perverse. You'd like a nuclear war.'

'I doubt it,' said Arlene. 'But I do like the rain. I like everything about it. I like the gentle drizzle of grey days. I like the pelting of storms.'

'And getting wet,' said Davy.

'That too. I don't mind that. It's better in the city, I think. I like rain in the countryside too, but it's better in the city.'

'Why?'

'You leave no footprints,' said Arlene. 'I mean, you do, but only for a few seconds. Then they're gone. Each footprint stays a moment, then it's gone.'

'There speaks a city girl,' I said.

Arlene ignored my subtle attempt to get her to reveal her origins.

'It can't always have been raining when I was small,' she said, 'but it feels that way. I think the rain must have entered my soul a long time ago. Now it kind of belongs there and I like it. I wouldn't want it any other way.'

'I'm going to take you to Florida,' said Davy.

'No thanks,' said Arlene. 'I prefer it here.'

Davy was right: Arlene was perverse. No one in their right mind would prefer this dump to Florida. The way I see it, Coney Island has lived in the collective memory like an ancient, comatose relative, incontinent and amnesiac, resident in the care home for longer than anyone can remember, but needing to be visited from time to time. Forget it. This was my first visit, and it will also be my last.

We were walking along Surf Avenue, a couple of hundred yards back from the shore. The stores were mostly closed, protected by metal roller-blinds covered in graffiti. That was the trouble with coming here at the start of the season: you couldn't tell how much of it was still closed for the winter, and how much was just closed. There were signs advertising premises to let. Grass sprouted between the slabs of the sidewalk. Abandoned premises bore Jewish names, or had signs in Cyrillic. Jews from before the state of Israel; Russians from the Revolution. Out there was the ocean that our families had crossed: the ocean that connected us to every other country, whose outcasts and misfits had created this one.

This was where we washed up, and at that point we

were simultaneously different and the same. How far did we now push on? It was a question of restlessness, I reckon. For some, that first voyage was enough: the coast of New York or New England was as far as they would get. Some pushed on till they reached the plains of the Midwest and made them their home. For others, that wasn't far enough. Nowhere was far enough until the Pacific imposed a last frontier. Or the Mexican border. Where you finally came to rest in your restlessness determined what sort of American you were. If you were on the east coast, the dust of Europe was on the soles of your feet. If you were on the west coast, or anywhere near it, you were living in a country of your own creation. Living where we do, I'm not sure to which country I belong.

'Darned gulls,' Davy said. 'Why don't they shut up? Why do they make that noise the whole time? Jesus. Can't even find peace at the seaside.'

No one else said anything.

'Don't you hate the screeching?' he said. 'Arlene? Aren't you fed up with it?'

'I sort of don't hear it,' she said.

'What do you mean, you don't hear it? How can you not hear it?'

'Well, I suppose I hear it. I just don't listen to it. There's lots of stuff I hear without listening.'

'Like what?'

'Like people getting wound up about gulls,' said Arlene. 'That's normal.'

'If you say so, Davy. I've no idea what normal is.'

We ate our hot dogs at Nathan's, the way everyone does. It's a compulsory experience. Afterwards, Marcie wanted to stroll and I didn't. Nothing unusual in that. You could tell the story of our married life through the subterfuges Marcie has adopted to get me to take some exercise, and the excuses I've invented to avoid it. It's not that I'm against exercise on principle. I used to play plenty of sports when I was younger. Nowadays, I'm on my feet most of the time I'm working, so I appreciate the opportunity to sit down.

'We went for a walk this morning,' I said.

'That lasted ten minutes,' said Marcie. Not true. It must have been a good two hours. 'I want to go along Brighton Beach and back.'

'I'll come with you,' said Davy.

That left Arlene. If she voted for a stroll, I'd have to go too. I never cared much for this winner-take-all democracy. Give me a pork barrel any time.

'I want to watch the ocean,' said Arlene. Marcie looked unimpressed.

'You can watch the ocean while we're walking,' said Davy.

'That's not the same thing. I want to sit down and stare at the ocean.'

So Marcie and Davy set off along the boulevard, and Arlene and I ambled to the boardwalk and found a bench. Arlene sat down.

'Is it OK if I sit next to you?' I asked. 'Or do you want time to yourself?'

'No, no,' said Arlene. She patted the damp wood next to her. 'Sit here. I don't need to be alone. I just want to look at the ocean.'

I sat on the bench a few inches apart from her and wondered if a conversation was in order, or if I should also contemplate the ocean in silence, in case it had a message to deliver.

'What are you thinking about?' I asked, after a few minutes.

'How small I am compared with this ocean. How insignificant.' Actually, that's not what she said. It's what I'd been expecting her to say, or something similar.

What she said was, 'Do you think you're the same person here as when you're at home?'

'Sure,' I said, 'I'm the same person anywhere. Aren't you?'

'I don't think so,' said Arlene. 'I think I'm many different people, depending on where I am. I think we all are.'

'What sort of person are you when you're here?'

'Here, I'm tranquil. I'm reflective. I'm poised. I'm in harmony with the world around me. I feel very small –' I knew she'd get that bit in – 'but proportioned.'

'A part of the universe,' I said.

'Exactly.'

'And what person are you when you're in my bar?'

54

'Then I'm a foetus,' said Arlene. 'I'm curled up within the womb of your world. I feel safe, but I don't feel a part of the universe. I'm a part of your universe, I guess. The one you and Marcie have created.'

'We haven't created anything. It happened.'

'Whatever.'

'And what person are you when you're at home?'

Arlene said nothing.

We sat there, contemplating something or other. I was contemplating the fact that Arlene had a habit of raising big existential questions and then clamming up. I'm not sure she was right, mind you. Or not right for me. I don't think I was any different on Coney Island than anywhere else. Nor Marcie. Maybe Arlene was different. I felt sorry for her. I think she raised questions like that in moments of a rare courage. She wanted to explain herself. She wasn't being enigmatic on purpose. In the end, the courage failed. Or else she couldn't explain herself.

'This is where Dreamland used to stand,' said Arlene. 'More or less.'

'The amusement park?'

'Yes.'

'Did they knock it down?'

'It knocked itself down. It was destroyed by fire. May 27, 1911. That was the night my family arrived here. As their boat came up Long Island Sound, their first sight of America was of Dreamland burning down.'

'You never came here as a kid?'

'No,' said Arlene. 'I've never been here. I've heard a lot about it, though. Coney Island's as real to me as many of the places I have been. That's why I wanted to come. I grew up on stories about Dreamland.'

'We all did.'

'I mean the real one. The one with a capital letter.' Arlene laughed. That is, she started to laugh, before remembering that laughing wasn't a thing she did much. 'I wonder if Freud and Jung sat on this bench,' she said. 'Like we're doing.'

'I didn't know they came here. Did they hold a psychologists' convention on Coney Island?'

'Maybe. They visited Dreamland together in 1909. Significant, don't you think?'

'If you're a psychologist, I expect everything's significant.'

Arlene ignored that remark. 'Freud said Coney Island was the only part of America that interested him.'

'Where else did he go?'

'New York city. Massachusetts. I think that was it.'

I thought Freud had made a damn fool comment in that case, but didn't like to say so. I was getting bored with this nebulous stuff, so I took the conversation somewhere more solid.

'I doubt Freud and Jung sat on this bench,' I said. 'I shouldn't think this bench existed in 1909.'

'I was speaking psychologically.'

'I was speaking factually. I didn't know benches could

be psychological. I don't know much about benches. And I know less about psychology.'

'I know too much,' said Arlene.

'Have you studied it?'

'Yes.'

'Where?'

'At college.'

'Where was that?'

'Out West. I flunked the course. Freud called America "a gigantic mistake". Did you know that?'

'No,' I said. 'I didn't know that.'

We sat in silence for another few minutes.

'Have you ever been unfaithful to Marcie?'

'For God's sake, Arlene. What sort of a question's that?'

'The sort of question no one asks,' she said. 'Have you?'

'No.'

'Has Marcie ever been unfaithful to you?'

'I don't believe so. Why don't you ask her?'

'I have,' said Arlene. 'She said she hadn't.'

'Well, there you are.'

'Why didn't you have children?'

'We did,' I said.

'And?'

'And nothing.' I've learned not to react when Marcie or I are asked that question. It took a long time. Now there is silence.

'I'm not the only one who won't talk about the past, am I?' said Arlene.

57

'You won't talk about the present,' I said.

Arlene smiled. 'Fair enough. So it's your turn. What do you want to ask me?'

'I've tried doing that,' I said. 'I don't get an answer. Nor does anyone else.'

'Try again.'

'Are you married?' I asked.

'No.'

'Never?'

'No.'

'Where do you live?'

'A little way out of town, at the moment.'

'On your own?'

'Yes.'

'Tell me about Jack,' I said.

Arlene sighed. She seemed about to say something, then stopped.

'I know you don't want to talk about it,' I said, 'and that's fine. But please give me a little to go on.'

Arlene sighed again.

'All right,' she said. 'I'll tell you a little, and a little's all I know. But I don't want you telling anyone else. You'll tell Marcie, I suppose, and that's all right. But no one else. Promise?'

'Promise.'

'Jack was a man . . . is a man . . . I'm not sure which . . . who used to send money to my mom.'

'Why would he do that?'

'I'm not sure yet.'

'Didn't your mom know?'

'I never knew about it till she was dead,' said Arlene. 'After that, the cheques kept coming. I had the same name as my mom, so I was able to bank them myself. I don't know whether I should have done, but I did. They stopped coming about three years ago.'

'And they were signed by Jack?' I asked.

'Yes.'

'Jack who?'

'Jack who indeed,' said Arlene. 'I've no idea. They were company cheques, so no one's name was printed. They still had to be signed, of course, and there was a great big Jack on each cheque. But the surname was illegible. Just a scrawl. I've taken it to handwriting experts and no one can tell me what it's meant to be.'

'Why do you think Jack lived in our town?'

'Postmarks,' said Arlene. 'But there were more than one of them.'

'So what do you believe?'

That was one question too many for Arlene. She had tired of revelations and wanted to retreat to a more familiar, more elusive world.

'What do I believe? I don't know. What can any of us believe? How can you believe what I've just told you? Maybe I made it all up. And how can I rely on what you've said?'

'Because it's true.'

Arlene pondered that reply.

'I didn't make friends when I was a kid,' she said. 'Not when I was young. Not when I was a teenager. Not when I was at college. Not for a while afterwards. I could have done. It's not that nobody wanted to be my friend. The fact is, I could never talk to people easily, so I didn't talk much at all. I think I was frightened of the world. I lived inside my own head. It was more comfortable for me, less scary. I don't expect this will surprise you. I imagine it's how you think I am now. It's what everybody thinks. In fact, I've got a lot better, but you're not to know that.

'The way we behave as kids is most truly how we are. Everything that comes after is a disguise, or an effort. It's a compromise between the person we are and the person the world needs us to be. When you've known someone as a child, you've known them from before the time they learned to dissemble. If they lied, you could see them lying, because they weren't smart enough to conceal it.

'There's nobody I know that well. Anyone I know, I've got to know a long time later. They were in their disguises when I met them, and I was in mine. It doesn't matter whether it's Davy, or you, or Marcie, or who it is. I don't know enough about you to know when you're telling the truth and when you're not, and you know as little about me. It doesn't matter what answers we give to questions. The answers cannot be believed, even if they're true.'

'I try to trust people until I find I can't,' I said.

'I'd like to do that.'

'Why don't you?'

Arlene stared out at the ocean, eyes fixed on the point where a probable sea met a debatable sky. A tear fell like a ripe plum on to her cheek, hesitated for a moment, then took the indirect route to her jaw.

'I'm sorry,' I said.

'Nothing for you to be sorry about.'

Arlene shrugged her shoulders. There was a long pause. I stood up, stretched my legs, took a few paces up and down. A little way off, Marcie and Davy advanced toward us down the boardwalk, deep in conversation, laughing.

'The others are coming,' I said to Arlene. I wanted to give her time to compose herself. She chose not to. She sat and stared at her horizon, or at some horizon she once had, old tears undried on her cheek, fresh ones forming.

'What's up, honey?' asked Davy. Marcie raised an eyebrow at me.

Her point was made, whatever point it might have been. Arlene dabbed her face, stood up and smiled.

'It kind of gets you, this place, doesn't it?' she said. Does it? It hadn't got me. Arlene made off toward the boulevard, Davy at her side. Marcie held back and we followed them at a distance.

'What upset Arlene?'

'I think she upset herself,' I said. 'I don't know why

someone would raise topics of conversation they know will disturb them. It doesn't make sense to me. That's the second time Arlene's made herself cry in front of an audience. I suppose she does it for effect.'

It was late afternoon and we had no more plans, except to go to a bar for the evening. Once we would have danced beneath a Coney Island moon, but there was nowhere left to dance. The next morning we'd be going home, back to a small town horizon. Had I enjoyed the jaunt? Yes, I suppose I'd enjoyed it. I think we all had. But home was real, and this wasn't. Give me real every time.

It was strange to be sitting in someone else's bar that night. In my own bar, I seldom drink alcohol. Here, I could have had as much as I wanted, but I didn't want any. I think the conversation with Arlene had flattened me. We were minus Davy. He said he'd got a headache and wanted to lie down in the hotel room. He might have had a headache. Or he could have been in some other part of Coney Island. Or have gone into Brooklyn or Manhattan for the evening. Or was hoping Arlene would say she had a headache too. Arlene came with us. It turned out that the afternoon's conversation with me had been an appetizer.

'Are you happy with your life?'

'Yes . . .' I began, then noticed that Arlene wasn't looking at me. She was asking the question of Marcie.

'What would you say?' Marcie threw the question back at her. She wasn't one for playing games.

'I'd say you were, but . . .'

'. . . but what?'

'It doesn't matter,' said Arlene. 'It really doesn't matter. It's a stupid question anyhow. Stones are easy to find if you're looking for pebbles. If you're looking for diamonds, it's harder.'

'What's that supposed to mean?' I asked.

'You think some of us set our standards too low,' said Marcie, shooting me another raised eyebrow.

'Oh, I didn't mean that. I was speaking generally. I wasn't suggesting for one moment that . . .'

Arlene was distressed to think she might have upset us. It occurred to me that she'd become fond of the pair of us. I don't know how old Arlene was. Coming up to forty, I'd say. Way too old to have been our daughter, for sure. But at times it was almost like she'd adopted us as parents.

'Are you happy with your life?' asked Marcie. It is one of her beliefs that people often ask the questions they want someone to ask of them.

'No. I don't think I am.'

'Why not?'

'I think I'm mediocre,' said Arlene. 'I don't think I've thought anything, felt anything, done anything, that millions of other people haven't thought, or felt, or done. There's nothing original about me.'

'Why does there need to be?'

'I don't see what the point is otherwise. I want to be

different. I want to do something unique and be remembered for it.'

'Still looking for diamonds on the beach,' said Marcie.

'I don't think there are any diamonds on the beach. I'm not sure there ever were.'

So we spent the evening: Arlene weaving pretty patterns with words, taking them, bending the words into arcs, the arcs into circles, while we wandered in circles around Arlene's world. To me, each loop was a blind alley, each circle a dead end. I'm a prosaic man and I deal with what's in front of me. I can't make up my mind if the ramblings of the enigmatics of this world come from a plane way above me, or if they're a load of baloney. I've never been able to decide that.

4

Come mid-May, other sightings of Franky Albertino were being reported around town. That's the thing about a place like this: it's large enough for events of interest to happen, depending on what you find interesting, I suppose, and small enough for individual comings and goings to get noticed. It's a place where people tend to stay. There's work nearby, and not just if you happen to run a bar or some local business. It's a safe place to raise a family. Lots of people who grow up here stay here for the rest of their lives. This is a roundabout way of saying that, when a ghost from the past arrives in town, he gets noticed. Not every ghost, I admit. Some people are barely noticed during the time they're here, so they can come back anytime they like, and no one's realized they ever left. Franky didn't fall into that category.

The guy from the hardware store said, would you believe it: Franky Albertino came in and bought a screwdriver. The lady from the grocery store on 4th said, would you believe it: Franky Albertino came in and bought a carton of milk. The priest from the Catholic church said, would you believe it: Franky Albertino came in and made his confession. Marcie told me that. I was amazed because, while Franky had been raised Catholic, he'd never been known to step inside the church since he got old enough to say boo to his parents. I was hoping Marcie would tell me what Franky had confessed, and how many hours it took. It turned out she was joking. She'd made the whole thing up.

As you'd expect, the two storekeepers pumped Franky as hard as they could for information, and got nothing back beyond the fact that he'd be hanging around for a while, living in a location undisclosed, for purposes that were similarly undisclosed. Mike said he'd seen him too, but had crossed the street to avoid him. He would have remembered Franky as well as any of us and was in no hurry to renew the acquaintance.

I half hoped he'd walk into the bar one evening, partly because I had a sneaking desire to see him, partly because it's harder to avoid questions in a bar than in a hardware store or at a checkout. The other half of me hoped he wouldn't. When Franky was around, trouble was never far behind. It was the second half of me that was satisfied for the time being. Franky didn't show up at the bar.

It was sometime in mid-May that Marcie fired the first salvo in the annual debate as to whether we would attend the County Fair together.

'So, are you coming this year?' she asked one evening.

She didn't need to say anything else. I knew what she meant.

We don't often attend the County Fair as a couple. It isn't held in our town so, although it's our county, it doesn't feel like our fair. Worse still, it's held in a town we've been at war with for decades, the bastard town I mentioned earlier. When I say 'war', I don't mean that anyone's been killed, but a few heads have got busted over the years, and a few egos even more so. The fact is they stole things from us. Important things. The court-house. The railroad station. A Carnegie library. These were ours until the thieving bastards purloined them by bribery and trickery and other violations of good neigh-bourly behaviour.

So we don't go there much. It's me that doesn't go, in fact. Marcie looks forward to the County Fair: it's an annual pilgrimage for her. She takes the attitude that it's stupid to hold crimes you barely understand against people you've never met, and to carry the grudge down the years. I tell her she misunderstands the nature of a good grudge. It gets better as the years wear on. The best grudges are the ones that have gone on so long no one can remember what started them. This grudge has centuries still to run.

Arlene said she wanted to go to the fair, not being from these parts. Davy said he wanted to go too, not being from these parts either, and wanting to be wher-ever Arlene was. Marcie didn't need persuading to say she'd go with them. And I thought I might as well tag along this year, although I'd rather not have had anything to do with the bastards. Possibly Arlene's company had something to do with that. So the four of us went off together, on the last Saturday in May.

We didn't have a fixed plan in mind, except to mosey round for a couple of hours, take some refreshment, and come home. Marcie wanted to see the farm equipment. It's not as if she's mechanically minded but, having grown up on a farm, whenever anything agricultural is in the vicinity, a primeval instinct homes her toward it. There was no keeping her away from the tractors. I think she'd have married a tractor if it had been legal. Arlene wanted to visit the rabbits. I told her she could do that at the pet store in town. That wasn't the same thing apparently, so Davy and I had to look at rabbits, and say how cute they were, while Arlene cuddled them.

Davy wandered off. I think he was irritated that Arlene cuddled the rabbits with more enthusiasm than she cuddled him. I could have told him that Marcie looked at tractors with more enthusiasm than she looked at me. After a while, I persuaded Arlene to abandon the rabbits and the two of us went off to find Davy. Along the way, we passed a guy, about my age, who smiled at us.

'Hiya, Arlene,' he said.

'Hiya.'

'Who was that?' I asked.

'Oh, just a guy I met at a bar in town,' said Arlene.

'In this town?'

'Yup.'

'I thought you had better taste,' I said. 'What are you doing drinking at a bar in this town? You're meant to be faithful to my bar.'

'I'm not faithful to any bar,' said Arlene. She pinched my arm. 'Now don't start getting jealous.'

When we found Davy, he was pounding a hammer at the Test Your Strength booth. Marcie soon joined us. Davy had stripped to the waist and was clattering the hell out of the machine. The three of us stood a little way off and watched. He was not the only man doing it. Beside him was another guy, early twenties maybe, also stripped to the waist. It looked like they were engaged in a contest, trying to see who could shoot the chaser highest up the pole. The guy who ran the booth stood at one side, counting the money.

'He'll give himself a heart attack if he goes on like that,' said Marcie. Arlene looked around distractedly and said nothing.

Davy was taking the contest with great seriousness. When it was his turn, he walked slowly up to the machine, blowing on his hands, gathering his concentration and his breath like he was an Olympic shot-putter. He threw his last ounce of strength into each blow. After each one, he sighed, whether out of satisfaction or disappointment being a moot point. His body glistened with sweat, and his veins bulged. The younger guy did the opposite. He never broke sweat. He sidled up to the machine, barely pausing before he smashed the hammer down. He had nearly turned away by the time the chaser reached its apex. He seemed disinterested in the proceedings, as if he did it to keep Davy amused and it was no big deal to him. He kept on going, though, just as Davy did.

The contest must have been about ten minutes old when we arrived. We didn't know who was winning or, in the end, who won, although that was immaterial by then. At the time, the three of us said little to each other. It was only afterwards, when Marcie and I were discussing it back home, that we realized we each had a different take on what we'd been watching. How is that possible? How can two people look at the same spectacle and disagree about what they're looking at?

It was my point of view that Davy was trying to prove he was as fit and strong as a man half his age and wouldn't accept nature's verdict. So he pounded away, with diminishing effect, clearly in a fury, raging against his own faded powers. The other guy kept his cool, not because he didn't care, otherwise why go on, but to emphasize the futility of the contest, and to rile Davy all the more.

Marcie didn't see it as a contest. She thought Davy and this other guy happened to have come to the booth at the same time and were taking turns at the hammer to give the other a rest. She didn't think they were competing with each other, or paying particular attention to how high they got the chaser.

'Why do you assume two men should be behaving like two women?' I asked her.

'Why do you assume everything in life is a trial of strength?'

'Because it is,' I said. 'Especially when two guys are doing something that advertises itself as a trial of strength.'

'Why weren't they talking to each other?' said Marcie.

'What was there to talk about, for Christ's sake? Waste of breath, and they needed all they had.'

I don't want you to think this was a serious dispute. Marcie and I don't have those. We keep a handful of arguments for special occasions, well rehearsed and pro- duced from time to time to keep us amused. By and large, I don't play the macho guy and I don't treat Marcie as the dumb blonde, specially since she's a brunette. She's also not dumb, and she may have been quite right in her view of what was going on. I'm not saying she wasn't.

Actually, I am saying that she wasn't.

I suppose guys aren't allowed to say things like that these days. We're allowed to think them, for the time being, but not to say them. I've no rooted objection to gender equality. If I'd wanted to marry a doormat, there's a good selection down the hardware store. Everyone says Marcie's a lot smarter than me. In fact, they don't say that either, but they think it. I think it myself. But sometimes I'm right. And even if I turn out not to be right, I regard it as my prerogative to make assertions. Marcie doesn't agree with that. She thinks you shouldn't make assertions when you're not sure of the facts. She asks questions instead.

After a strike of massive exertion, Davy slid down the front of the machine, his back resting against it. Marcie was the first to see that anything was wrong. She gave a small cry and rushed toward him. She'd been right: he'd given himself a heart attack. Before long, there were paramedics everywhere and he was being carted off to the nearest hospital. Fortunately, that was close by. The thieving bastards had stolen that from our town as well.

Davy must have been mid-forties at this time. Despite what I've said, he was fit, just not as fit as a twenty-something. The attack had not been severe, it turned out, and Davy recovered from it quickly. He was in hospital for a few days and we went to visit him. For some reason Arlene didn't. I think she went away for a while. Davy came back with a load of pills to reduce his blood pressure, which was a bonus. It didn't take a heart attack, or a doctor, to spot that Davy's blood pressure was way too high. On the face of it, everything went back to normal pretty quickly.

Except it didn't. Davy appeared to decide that he was now middle-aged, or at least not young anymore. He took a conscious decision to age. Davy knew who he was

72

before. He was hot-headed and irritable, which was annoying sometimes, but it gave him character. He conveyed the impression of being mad at what had happened in an earlier life. He seemed to want to begin a new life, and to have chosen Arlene as part of the makeover. At least, that's what we thought at the time.

The new post-heart attack Davy had no idea who he was, and if he didn't, we sure as hell didn't either. He was trying on bits of a new persona as if he was trying on items of clothing, and few of them fitted. The things that used to rile him, riled him no longer. Or rather, they did rile him, but he tried not to show it. As a result, he became irritating, because we were always conscious that he was trying to suppress stuff.

At some point, this began to have an effect on Arlene. When we get attracted to someone, we are attracted to the image they present of themselves, which is seldom the complete reality. If it's close enough to the reality, it won't make a difference. We expect a few things to come creeping out of other people's closets when we're no longer star blinded by them. In Davy's case, what you saw was pretty close to what you got, or it had been until then.

Things started to change between Davy and Arlene. There had never appeared to be much passion in the relationship, so far as we could tell. It was like their fire had been lit with damp wood. But the conversations had been animated, at least on Davy's part. On Arlene's side, less so, it seemed. Now Davy was no longer animated, and there were longer silences. You could say that they ran out of things to talk about, but Davy had never had much to talk about. He just talked. And Arlene listened, most of the time. But you can't listen to someone who's not saying anything. For a while, they continued to sit together. I saw the glances, the glances away from each other, the glances that searched for a more interesting conversation elsewhere in the bar, the glances of disengagement.

They stopped huddling in their corner. They wandered round the bar, joining other conversations. They stopped singing. Eventually Arlene began to come in less often and Davy appeared not to mind. You could say that she'd got bored with him, but I don't think that was it. Arlene had got bored with herself, which is another way of saying she had got bored with life.

'Davy shouldn't have tried to reinvent himself,' I said to Marcie one night.

'I don't think that was the cause of it,' said Marcie. 'It happened before then. You and I watched it happen in front of us.'

'When was that?'

'At the County Fair. Before the heart attack. When Davy was straining every sinew on the machine, and Arlene stood there, looking bored, looking away, looking for someone else.'

'And?'

'Something clicked in her. It was almost audible. It had to do with seeing the two men at the machine, side by side. I think it reminded her of Davy's age, and of her own age too. I've been looking at the two of them these past months, and it doesn't look right. I can see Arlene with a man half her age, or with one twice her age. But not with a man who's close to her own age. That's too much for her. Arlene's terrified of getting old.'

We spent so much time last year discussing Arlene, analysing Arlene, trying to work out the mystery of Arlene. And, of course, trying to work out the mystery of Jack. Two enigmas for the price of one. Arlene draped a magician's cloak around the sanctum of her soul and left the world to guess what lay behind it. Possibly nothing much lay behind it. A jumble of neuroses and insecurities, some bad memories, the unreasonable hope that someone else would come along and do for her what she couldn't do for herself. Outside, Arlene was the polished lacquer of a bamboo stem; inside, she was a series of hollow chambers, each insulated against the next. Christ, that sounds bitchy. It means, I suppose, that Arlene was much like the rest of us. She looked different. We wanted her to be different. In the end, she turned out to be the same, in a different way. And we were disappointed because we had expectations, and we had those because we were bored, and wanted something new to happen, like she did.

As for Davy, I couldn't say. I struggle to know the

friends I've had all my life. At times, I struggle to know Marcie. I never met Davy in his previous incarnation, so I can't tell you how Davy Mark II differed from Davy Mark I. And now here was Davy Mark III. My guess is that Davy suffers from low self-esteem, camouflaged by a lot of noise and dogmatic assertion. I reckon that, when he met Arlene and when Arlene took to him, he began to have a better opinion of himself. Then, when Arlene seemed to lose interest, Davy thought that it must be his fault, that his original evaluation of himself had been correct.

What goes through our heads at times like these is such baloney, isn't it? In our own estimation, we go from superhero one second to poor damned fool the next, with no stopover. As far as I could see, Davy and Arlene were good for each other. They got along great until these stupid mind things got in the way. They'd both had big disappointments. At least, we assumed they had. We thought, this is meant to be; this is their break; this is the time they put their pasts behind them and get on with the future. Maybe we always hope that for other people's relationships. As well as for our own.

I suppose only psychopaths get to put their pasts behind them. The rest of us carry them around with us, lumbered on our backs, swollen with the rainfall of the years. There's no refuge from the weight of the past. It seeps into crevices we don't know exist, and poisons the wells at which we hope to drink. Even if we're not jealous, our pasts are jealous on our behalf, demanding fidelity, requiring us to be true to them unto death. The future doesn't get a look-in. So it gets bored and goes off to flirt with someone else, and the same thing happens all over.

Now I look at what I've said about the County Fair, and how it changed Davy and Arlene and their relationship, I'm not sure I agree with it. What I've said is what Marcie and I concluded at the time, based on what we knew at the time. Afterwards, a lot happened that changed our minds about many things. That should have made us revisit our attitude to the fair and its aftermath. Somehow it hasn't. There's no doubt that Davy and Arlene's relationship changed around that time. It now occurs to me there could have been several explanations for that fact, apart from the one I've given.

Anyhow, the County Fair stands out for me. It was the last act of a spring that had been full of drama, and the first act of a summer that would be fuller still. At any rate, we knew it was the day that summer began. The County Fair publicity said so. Who could fail to believe the lying bastards next door?

5

One evening in the middle of June, a couple of weeks or so after the fair, Franky Albertino walked into the bar. It was around six o'clock. A few of the way-home-from-work crowd were downing a fortifier to cleanse the day and prepare their psyches for reunion with wives and children. Steve had called in sick, so Marcie would have to help me out in a while. In the meantime, she'd gone upstairs to rest her feet. I was cleaning up in a desultory sort of way. Franky couldn't have chosen a better time to find me nearly on my own, if that was what he wanted, which it probably was.

'Hello, Franky. Long time no see. Want a beer?'

'Why not?' He moved as if to get some cash from his pocket.

'No need for that,' I said. 'First one's on the house.'

'Thanks,' said Franky. 'I'll pay all the same, if you don't mind. Don't want to get the reputation of a scrounger.' He smiled, in a charming sort of way.

I didn't pretend to be surprised to see him, and he didn't pretend to be surprised that I wasn't surprised.

Franky knows what gossip's like in this town. He didn't look much different from the last time I'd seen him. Short, straight hair, still jet black, unless he dyed it. The same crooked grin, which suited in more than one respect. The same cherubic features, which didn't.

'Good to have you back,' I said, not yet sure I was feeling that way toward him, but being used by now to welcoming anyone who came in to spend good money.

'Yeah,' said Franky. He gulped a draught of his beer, then took a long look round the place. 'Nice joint you've got yourself here.'

'Thanks.'

'Never figured you for a barkeeper.'

'No? What did you figure me for?'

'I thought you'd become a teacher.'

'I did for a while. Now I'm doing this. What are you up to these days?'

'Oh, you know,' said Franky.

'Are you working?'

'I buy a bit of this, sell a bit of that.'

'You're a dealer,' I said.

'Yeah, I guess that's it. I'm a dealer.' Dealing what? Automobiles? Drugs? Low blows to all and sundry? Franky wasn't about to be more specific.

'And what brings you back to town?'

'Business brought me nearby,' he said, 'and I had this notion to come back and see how the place was and who was still here. Curiosity, I suppose.'

The man who runs the real-estate outfit on Main Street had supplied details of another sighting of Franky in town. He'd told me that Franky had come in to enquire about properties, so there seemed to be some sort of plan. He'd given his current address as a motel on the other side of town. More information would be forthcoming in due course, no doubt. There were plenty of people around who remembered Franky and would be wondering what he was up to, fearing that the general answer would be 'no good'.

'Have you seen anyone since you've been back?'

'A few,' said Franky. 'Not to talk to much. Fact is, I get a little confused as to who everyone is. I recognize people, or think I do, but I can't place them exactly. I don't want to put my foot in it.'

'Never stopped you before, Franky,' I said. I might have mentioned that his foot was not the only part of his anatomy he put in it, but that would have been antagonistic, not to mention crude.

Franky laughed. 'No one lives down their past, do they? I leave here thirty years ago, and I come back and it's like thirty minutes. The things I did then, I did yesterday. The guy I was then, I am now.'

'I expect you think the same of us,' I said.

'I expect I do. I was making a general point, not being personal.' He seemed defensive, no longer sure of his place in the scheme of things. He didn't used to be that way. He was cock of the roost once, and knew it better than anyone.

'So you haven't looked anybody up?'

'Not yet.' He looked round the bar again. 'Not yet.' If Franky wanted to see someone, he'd need to know if they were in town and where they lived, and he would need to ask. It didn't sound like he'd asked anyone else, so I thought he'd ask me. He didn't.

'Funny old life,' was all he said for the moment. I left him to his drink and went to serve another customer. While I was doing it, Marcie came into the bar.

'Hello, Franky. Imagine seeing you here.'

'Hi, Marie.'

'Marcie. As you know.'

'Oh, yeah. Hi, Marcie.' He looked puzzled. 'What are you doing here?'

Marcie didn't give the obvious answer for the moment. 'Why shouldn't I be here? Isn't a girl allowed to have a drink?'

'Oh, sure,' said Franky. 'Of course you are. It was just that . . .'

'. . . just what?'

'Just that I imagined you'd be married.'

'I am,' said Marcie.

'Oh,' said Franky.

'To me,' I said.

'Oh, right,' said Franky. 'I get it. I'd forgotten the two of you used to be an item. You run this place together.'

'You got it,' said Marcie.

'Well, who'd have thought it?' said Franky. 'Who'd have thought it?' He shook his head slowly. Marcie looked at me and raised an eyebrow. 'Who'd have thought it?' said Franky again.

'It's been over a quarter of a century,' I said. 'You can't think that nothing's changed.'

'I know that,' said Franky. 'I've changed, for a start.'

'So has everyone else,' said Marcie.

'How have you changed?' I asked.

'I'm older.'

'Amazing,' said Marcie.

'And wiser?' I asked.

Franky laughed. 'I don't think I was born to be wise,' he said. 'I think I was born to make every darned mistake known to man, one after the other.'

It sounded as if we might soon learn something. You can pack a load of mistakes into thirty years. Just then, Arlene came through the door. She greeted Marcie and me in an absent-minded way, gave the impression of ignoring Franky, and looked around the bar.

'Where's Davy?' she asked. 'Has he been in?'

'No,' I said. 'Not yet.'

'Are you sure?' said Arlene. 'We were meant to meet twenty minutes ago. I'm running late.'

'He's running later,' said Marcie.

Arlene was always running late. In fact, I can't remember another instance when she turned up before

Davy. Their meetings had appeared to happen by accident. And now that the two of them were winding down as a couple, they weren't happening much at all. That evening, Arlene decided to attach herself to us. I made the introductions.

'Arlene, this is Franky. He used to live in town years ago.'

'Hi, Arlene,' said Franky. 'Can I get you a drink?'

For a moment, Arlene weighed up the offer. Then she said, 'Vodka Martini, please.'

'My lucky day,' said Franky. 'Come in here to see an old friend, and this gorgeous lady walks in.'

'Why, thank you,' said Arlene.

'How do you know he wasn't talking about me?' asked Marcie.

I don't know how people like Franky get away with it. The point is they do. He didn't make that remark to Arlene, not directly. He was looking at me as he said it, giving me a wink. I don't know if he'd missed the bit about Arlene waiting for Davy, or had decided to ignore it. I sensed Marcie bristling next to me. Arlene smiled in a demure sort of way.

She was sitting on her stool at the bar, and Franky was sitting next to her. In fact, he was sitting on Davy's stool, not that he could have known that, although it was typical that he should have chosen it. Looking at the two of them together, they seemed perfectly matched, physically. I expect anthropologists have a classification for it.

If Arlene was Caucasian female, type 3, Franky was Caucasian male, type 3. Pleasant, balanced features. Perfect teeth. A similar smile, slightly crooked, more frequently bestowed by Franky. Mid-length black hair in Arlene's case; short black hair in Franky's. The eyes differed, though. Arlene's were so dark they were nearly black. Franky's were brown. Both were well dressed, right down to their feet. Franky had always been particular about his footwear, even at school. Now he was wearing a pair of tan-and-white spectator shoes, which made him look the proper lounge lizard.

If an anthropologist would lump the two of them together, a psychologist would not. Knowing them as well as I did, it's easy for me to say that, but I think anyone could see it from looking at them. There was no mistaking the fact that one was an introvert and the other an extrovert. However, they did have one trait in common. Neither was open about themselves. Arlene did it by non-disclosure; Franky, unless he'd changed, did it by disclosing inaccurate information. It was easy to spot the type of person that each of them was, but not the specific person. That was kept well hidden in both cases.

Franky looked at Arlene. 'Shall we go and find a table somewhere?' he asked.

'It's OK,' said Arlene. 'I'm fine here.' Her eyes were jammed on to Franky's, and she didn't repeat that she was waiting for someone. She wanted to be with Franky, but she wanted chaperones.

'I hear you're staying at the Carradine Motel, Franky,' I said.

'For the time being, yeah.'

'How do you find it?'

'Same as any other place. The bed's good and comfortable, anyway.' He was glancing at Arlene's chest as he said this. She seemed to find it amusing.

'What do you want from us, Franky?' Trust Marcie to get to the heart of the matter in a short time.

'What do you mean, what do I want from you?'

'Like I say. What do you want from us?'

'I don't know,' said Franky. 'I don't think I want anything in particular. Why do you assume I should want something?'

'Because you always did,' said Marcie.

'We all want something,' said Arlene.

'Do we? What do you want?'

'What I want is a hero,' said Arlene. 'A twenty-four-carat, rock-solid hero.'

'I'm your man,' said Franky.

'No, he isn't,' said Marcie.

'What sort of hero do you have in mind?' asked Franky.

'I don't know,' said Arlene. 'A regular guy type hero. Not a man who's in love with money. Not a man who's aiming for win, place or show in the rat race. Not a man who's eyeing the next car, the next house, the next woman.'

'I asked what sort of hero you wanted,' said Franky. 'Not what sort you didn't.'

'All right. I want someone who seems totally ordinary, then turns out not to be. Someone who will step up to the plate when the flash guys have chickened out.'

'I knew you weren't the man,' said Marcie.

Franky was about to lob a remark back at her, then thought better of it. That happened a few times while he was in town. The trouble with guys like Franky is they don't have much of a memory for the things they do to other people. They do them, then they move on. If you're on the receiving end, you don't forget it. What Franky did to people in this town was done thirty years ago or more, so he would have remembered less. At the time, I thought Franky took the view that it would be wiser not to provoke Marcie into recalling something that he might have forgotten.

All through this encounter, I had the feeling that I was watching the performance of a private drama between Arlene and Franky. Marcie had the same feeling, I discovered later. It was like they were acting out a script they'd written together. Yet they were strangers. When I introduced them, they were meeting for the first time, I could swear to it. By the end of the conversation, they'd known each other for years. This isn't a loose way of saying it was love at first sight, although it might have been that as well. It was a mutual recognition of something.

We had Franky, a renegade from this town, and

Arlene, an enigma from anywhere except here. Two people who had never met, who seemed to make sense to the other and to no one else. I said this to Steve later, and to Mike and Nelson, and they didn't buy it. They thought I was imagining it. Or perhaps that Franky and Arlene had once had a fling, and wanted to act like they hadn't. I don't think any of that was true.

Davy came in at this point. He looked around, saw Arlene, headed toward us. Then he hesitated, then started toward us again. Franky shadowed off, making as if he was inspecting the electricity supply.

'Hi, honey,' said Davy. 'Sorry I'm late. Why don't we go someplace else tonight?'

He didn't wait for an answer, took Arlene by the arm and led her to the door. Arlene looked back and shrugged her shoulders, as if to say she didn't know what was going on, but what the hell. Davy and Arlene never went anyplace else. Davy never failed to acknowledge Marcie or myself, to say good evening to us. Things were disjointed that night. Davy apologized afterwards, said the vibe hadn't been good.

Franky hung around for a short while, not saying much, then he left as well.

'See you around, guys.'

'See you around, Franky,' I said.

Marcie kept her mouth shut until he was through the doors. Then she said, 'I'd forgotten quite how obvious he is.'

She had a point. Franky Albertino was obvious. When we were kids, we didn't realize that, except for Marcie, of course. Or perhaps we liked it. After all, there's nothing so obvious as a comedian with a good catchphrase, and people go on laughing. We were constantly taken in by Franky. We were learning about people, and about life. The obvious wasn't obvious, in those days. Looking at Franky when he came back, it seemed unbelievable that he had taken us in for a second. It could be that we'd become wiser, or that Franky had got more obvious still. He acted older than we did back then. Now he acted younger. As a general rule, it's good to act your age.

Marcie disliked Franky, as you may have gathered. I didn't know whether there was a specific reason for this, or if she simply disliked him the way most other people did. It hadn't mattered before now. There might have been a story I'd once been told and had now forgotten. Or maybe there hadn't been a story. I decided to play it safe and act as if I knew, which is tough if you don't know, and are worried you'll say the wrong thing and put your foot in it, while hoping that at some point you'll be given a clue as to what it is you've forgotten, assuming you were ever told, and can then give the impression of having known all along.

'Some nerve coming back, after the way he left,' Marcie said.

'Yes,' I said. Be more specific, woman, if you please. But she wasn't.

'He'll be in town for a reason. And he'll be back here before long to bend you into helping him.'

'Why should he want to do that?'

'Because Franky always asked for help and you never refused it. You couldn't say no to Franky. You managed to see a good side to him after he'd done a hundred and one pirouettes and no one else could see one.'

'Possibly.'

'It's OK, honey,' said Marcie. 'It's not a criticism. It was noble of you, in a way. It's just that you were wrong.' As a verdict, I settled for that. 'Noble, but wrong' was good in the circumstances. It could have been a lot worse and maybe yet would be.

I can't disagree with Marcie's assessment of Franky, but you've got to hand it to the guy for livening things up. Life's never dull when Franky's around. Since tedium is public enemy number one, that's saying plenty. Personally, I was glad he was back in town, even if I had to finesse that view around the house, especially after what happened a week or two later.

Marcie and I had retired for the night after an unmemorable evening. Outside, it was blowing a gale. I couldn't get to sleep for a while, what with the wind rattling the casements, and I'd only just nodded off when there came a bang, bang, bang from the general direction of the front door. You know how it is in situations like that. You're barely awake and you don't want to make yourself any more awake, in case you can't get back to sleep, so you convince yourself of things you know to be baloney. Bang. Must have imagined it. Ignore it. Bang. Must have got tangled up with a dream. Ignore it. Bang. Goddamned wind. Maybe I forgot to close the porch screen. Ignore it. Bang. No use. Somebody's there. Who would come calling at two in the morning? No one I'd want to see. Ignore it. Bang.

'Aren't you going to find out who it is, honey?' I hadn't suspected Marcie of being awake. She's too good at playing possum.

Marcie was not planning on going herself. It's a man's job to deal with people who come calling in the middle of the night. The tide of gender equality has come rolling up the foreshore, but it hasn't left a neat line. It has grabbed the easy pickings, like money, and left others untouched. Physical danger, for example. I'm not making a big deal of it. I'm just saying. Anyway, now there was nothing for it. I had to go to the front door. On the other side of it stood Franky, soaking wet, dishevelled, suffering from assorted abrasions to head and arms.

'What the hell, Franky?' I said. 'You'd better come in.'

I sat him down at the kitchen table and went to fetch Marcie. Yes, I know. Nursing has remained a female preserve in our household. I wouldn't have had a clue what to do. My medical cabinet consists of a bottle of bourbon. The following twenty minutes or so were a pastiche of gender stereotyping. Female acquired bandages and plasters and disinfectant and bottles of lotions and hot, soapy water, and set about bathing and dressing the wounds of male number one, cooing while she did it, even though she detested him. Male number one who, to be factual, had nothing much wrong with him, winced at every touch and sucked in air through clenched teeth. 'Thhhhhhhh,' he went, 'thhhhhhhh.' As if he was brave as hell and had survived a war. Male number two produced the bottle of bourbon, poured two glasses, wafted the bottle in the direction of the female, who shook her head puritanically, and proceeded to talk to male number one about the sports results.

Franky got patched up. He began to concentrate less on his ailments and more on the bourbon. He remembered to thank Marcie for her ministrations. Then he started making moves to go. Oh, no. Not yet, Franky. We need to get something out of this. You're not leaving till you've told us what the hell you've been up to.

'Had a bit of bother, that's all,' said Franky.

'We can see that. What happened?'

'Got in a scrap.'

I've seen a few scraps over the years, and I know the sorts of injury that result from them. Franky's didn't come from a scrap.

'Where was that? You been fighting in our parking lot?'

'No,' said Franky. 'It was a distance away. You were the nearest people I could think of. I thought you might be up. Sorry.'

'We're not normally up at two in the morning,' I said. 'Who are you in the habit of fighting at this hour?'

'No one in particular.'

Most people don't lie, or not much. When they do, they get embarrassed, and give themselves away, and change the subject as quickly as they can. Habitual liars don't do that. They carry on lying as if it's the most natural thing in the world, which for them it is. Franky is a habitual liar. He would have gone on like this for an hour or more if we'd let him. Marcie didn't let him.

'Why were you climbing a tree out the back here in the middle of the night?'

Franky looked rattled. I don't think he was expecting to be believed, but he wasn't expecting to be contradicted. Still, Franky didn't get to be a seasoned liar by conceding ground to the enemy.

'Look,' he said, 'I'm grateful to you for patching me up. I'd like to be getting home now, if you don't mind. It's late.'

'We're aware of that,' said Marcie. 'How are you planning on getting home?'

'Got a car outside.'

'In our parking lot?'

'Yeah.' There was no way out of that one.

'Do you normally drive to your sporting fixtures?' I asked.

'It's a complicated story,' said Franky. 'I'll tell you some other time.'

And with that, he was gone. We heard a car start up and drive away. Marcie and I looked at each other and returned to bed.

'How did you know he was climbing a tree?'

'I heard him,' said Marcie. 'Must have been one of the trees on the edge of Mr Hammond's property. I heard a rustling of the branches. I heard a snapping of twigs as he lost his footing. I heard the thump as he landed.'

'Why would Franky be climbing one of Mr Hammond's trees in the middle of the night? What was he hoping to see?'

'It's like I said before,' said Marcie. 'Franky's back in town for a reason. Franky Albertino doesn't do anything without a reason. I expect we'll get to find out what it is one of these days. I suspect it's got to do with Mr Hammond.'

'Or with his house.'

'Yes. Or that. Do you remember there being anything between the Albertinos and Mr Hammond?'

'No,' I said. 'I don't.'

'I'm sure there was something,' said Marcie. 'I don't remember what it was. Maybe it'll come back to me. It was one of my frustrations when I was a child. Adults discussed things that I couldn't understand. I knew the words, and I knew what they meant, but I didn't understand the conversation.'

6

It was a while before we knew that Arlene and Davy had parted. We had suspected it; we had debated it when Davy wasn't there; but it was nearly three weeks before we knew. That was because Davy gave an Oscar performance in the role of normal Norman.

The first few days after his exit with Arlene, the night that Franky was in the bar, Davy didn't come in. He was probably at home taking it out on the cat, not that he had a cat. Nothing unusual about his absence. A few days often went by without Davy or Arlene showing up. By the time he did come in, Davy had composed himself. He smiled at everyone, bought us drinks and had conversations. He didn't go and reserve himself a table like he did when he was waiting for Arlene; otherwise he was the same as ever. He acted like he hadn't noticed that Arlene wasn't there, so we acted that way too. Because Davy behaved as if her absence was natural, we assumed it must be. Maybe she was ill, or had needed to go away somewhere.

By the end of week two, we felt like we should be

saying something. She was a friend of ours as well. Not to ask after her would sound like indifference. But asking after someone implied they were no longer around, which would be abnormal, and Davy was busy advertising the fact that nothing was abnormal, so we hesitated. One day I found the courage.

'How's Arlene, Davy?'

'She's good.' Pause. 'Far as I know.'

'Gone away somewhere for a while?'

'Possibly. I can't say. Haven't seen much of her recently.'

'Sorry to hear that,' I said. 'Will we be seeing her again?'

'You'd have to ask her.'

'A little difficult as she's not here.'

And that was that. Goodbye, Arlene. We had no idea what had happened. Davy wasn't saying more than he needed to, and he didn't need to say anything. It was no one else's business.

I had a friend who got divorced after a few years of marriage. He and his wife had been childhood sweethearts, inseparable since they were knee high, and therefore cursed by the world's expectations, their own included. They would have been friends for life if they hadn't married. That's not the point I'm making, however, although it's interesting as a by-the-by. The point is that this guy had loads of pictures of his wife, as a kid, as a teenager, on their wedding day, in married life:

dozens of pictures, in frames and in albums, scattered around the house.

When they divorced, he destroyed the lot of them. The frames were saved, because he was a skinflint and they might come in handy for wives two, three and four. He placed the images of his ex-wife in a pile in the garden and invited some of his friends round. His male friends, I mean; I'm not sure he had any other kind. He cracked open a few beers, poured barbecue fuel on the photos and had a bonfire. I've seldom seen anyone look so happy. If you can have referred pain, I imagine you can have referred murder.

I didn't approve of this behaviour, and said so. I told him he was no better than the Soviets, changing their street names as soon as someone fell out of favour, pretending that yesterday's hero had never existed. I didn't expect him to keep framed pictures in the house. That would have been masochism. It was the wholesale destruction I objected to, and the belief that if you destroyed the image, you destroyed the person, and thereby any role they might have played in your life. You shouldn't rewrite history, in my opinion. Things that happened, happened. Things that didn't happen, didn't happen. Maintaining a distinction between the two is fundamental.

I'm getting distracted here. What I wanted to say is that Davy's attitude to splitting up with Arlene was reminiscent of my friend's attitude to his ex-wife. If

Davy had photos of Arlene, they'd have been destroyed also. She never happened, thank you very much. Did you say the two of us had an affair for several months? I don't think so. Where's the evidence for that?

In any case it didn't last, Davy's odd behaviour over Arlene. How could it? He was a hothead at heart. Soon after my surreal conversation with him, normal Norman reverted to normal Davy. He scowled in one evening and sat at a table with a beer, acting as if he was morose. That's because he was morose, but he was also acting it. He wanted everyone to know he was morose. He was doing method school of morose.

I stood a few feet away, hands on hips, Marcie style, and smiled at him. Not a big smile. What I thought was a sympathetic smile. I was hoping to have achieved the right compromise of attitude.

'What are you staring at?'

'Want another beer, Davy?'

'I can ask if I do.'

'Shall I set up a drink for Arlene?' That was provocative on my part, but I don't like to be treated that way by anyone.

'Shithead.' Davy slammed down his empty glass, got up and stomped out of the bar. A few seconds later we heard the screech of the wheels. The tyres were method acting too. Some joker went and put 'My Guy' on the jukebox.

The next evening, Davy came in as if nothing was

wrong. He sat at the bar with Nelson, and the three of us exchanged the day's news. Some people feel awkward after an outburst and want to make amends. Others behave as if it never happened. Davy belonged in the latter category.

'You guys will be seeing a lot more of me now,' he said.

'Why's that?'

'Arlene's gone.' We had the official confirmation. It's hard to describe Davy's demeanour as he said that. There wasn't any feeling in it. The previous night he'd been angry. Now he was . . . I don't know. Indifferent.

'That's tough,' said Nelson. 'Did the two of you have a bust-up?'

'Not as far as I know. She just went. Left a note to say she was going, and went.'

'Where to?'

'She said she was going to Indiana. Gone looking for Jack again. Maybe she has; maybe she hasn't. I haven't a clue. Don't know where she came from. Don't know where she's gone.'

If Arlene had left Davy a note, she'd left it at Davy's place, unless she'd pushed it under his car wiper. We hadn't known where Arlene and Davy used to go when they left the bar. We assumed it would have been his apartment, but it might not have been.

'Where does she live?' asked Nelson.

'I never found out.'

'You dated for three months and you don't know where she lives?'

'That's right.'

'Did you ask?'

'Of course I asked,' said Davy. 'Asked her where she lived. Asked her whether she was married. Asked her where she came from. Asked her the same questions you've asked, and got the same responses.'

'So you don't know her any better than we do,' said Nelson.

'I wouldn't say that. In some respects, I know her very well. It's just that I don't know the answers to those particular questions.'

'I never liked her,' said Nelson. 'Too tarty for my taste.'

That was a dumb remark in any circumstance. It was also bullshit, given Nelson's own attempt to pick up Arlene. I braced myself for Davy's reaction and calculated whether I was fit enough to get over the bar and separate them, if it came to it. It didn't come to it. Davy didn't rise to the bait. I wondered if he was under sedation.

'She's not tarty,' said Davy. 'She looks it, I grant you, but she's not. In a way, she's quite strait-laced. There's something old-fashioned about her. She belongs to more innocent times.'

Marcie chose that moment to join me behind the counter. She sometimes comes down in the evening if there's nothing to watch on TV, especially when there's gossip around. Her antennae are tuned that way. Mike came in about the same time and I filled them both in on the evening's news. Nelson was in the middle of telling Davy he was well out of it.

'You may be right,' said Davy, 'although I can't see how you'd know.'

'I've lived a bit,' said Nelson.

We've all lived a bit. Davy as much as Nelson, and Marcie and me more than both of them. It doesn't make you wiser if you're not wise to start with, and Nelson had no reputation for wisdom.

'You saying that Arlene's gone?' Mike sounded puzzled.

'That's right,' said Davy.

'Well, she hasn't gone far. I saw her in town today.'

'Really?' I said. 'That's a first. Whereabouts?'

'She was getting out of her car near the Carradine Motel.'

I tried to remember who I'd told that Franky was staying at the Carradine. No one, I thought. Only Marcie and myself knew. And Arlene, of course. None of the others reacted to Mike's news.

'We haven't seen the last of Arlene,' said Nelson.

'What makes you say that?' Davy didn't seem animated at the prospect, merely curious. 'Is that what you think, Marcie?'

'I don't know,' said Marcie. 'Sometimes a wildcat

comes back to the same farm. Sometimes not. We're acting as if this is to do with you, Davy. Maybe it's to do with Jack.'

'Well, she's certainly got us talking about her,' said Mike. 'If that's what she wants.'

'Who knows what Arlene wants,' said Davy.

'You seem pretty calm,' I said.

'Thanks,' said Davy. 'I appreciate you saying that.'

'A lot calmer than last night,' I said, in case he'd forgotten.

'Yeah. Well. I've had a day of anger-management therapy now.'

'What does that consist of?'

'It's a cut-price therapy,' said Davy. 'One part punch-bag at the gym. One part tranquillizers. One part crate of beer. And an ice pack afterwards. It works great.'

'Must really help with self-knowledge,' said Nelson.

'What the hell would you know about that?' I don't know how you put a smile into a sentence, but Davy put a big smile into that one.

'I reckon I've got it worked out,' he went on. 'Figured it to a T.' He nodded his head several times to show that he agreed with himself. We weren't nodding. 'Went down to the gym this morning. Had a real good workout. Came back and lay on the sofa with a handful of beers and the pills, and figured it all out.'

'What did you figure?' asked Marcie.

'Everything.'

'Such as?'

'I need to be more assertive,' said Davy. 'Not aggressive. Assertive. I've been confusing the two. I've never known how to be assertive before now. That's why I get aggressive. That's why I hit people.'

'You still hit people?' I said. 'I thought that was just your calling card when you first came here.'

'I've always hit people,' said Davy. 'I've come to expect it of myself.' He shook his head slowly. Maybe he was now disagreeing with himself.

Davy had been half standing, elbow on the edge of the counter, and half sitting, backside on the edge of his high stool. Now he slid off. The elbow was the first to lose tenure, followed by the rest of him. The stool collapsed behind, and Davy collapsed on to it. He was out for the count, briefly. I fetched a jug of water and splashed it over his face until he came round.

'You should take care of your surfaces,' he said. 'A good lawyer would make mincemeat out of this joint.'

'Are you all right?' asked Marcie.

'Yeah. Now where was I?'

Davy was not all right. I didn't think he'd done himself serious damage, but he was not all right. I can usually spot the warning signs with the regulars. Drink takes each of them in a different way, but it takes them. Davy was the hardest to spot. He'd give the impression of being sober until the moment he hit the ground. It had happened three or four times in the past. Each time it caught me by surprise. I should learn to pay attention to his calmness: it's not natural to him and it means he's smashed.

'It's time to go home,' I said.

'It's OK,' said Davy. 'I'm fine. Just slipped, that's all. Time for another beer, Mr Bartender, please. And one for my good friends here.' He waved his arm in the general direction of Mike and Nelson.

These are the moments I dread. I'm happy to take anyone's money most of the time, but the job comes with responsibilities, and one of them is not pouring alcohol down the throat of someone who's already had too much. I didn't know how Davy would take that news. The short fuse seemed to have lengthened a few feet in the last day, but I didn't trust it not to shrink again without notice. I wasn't sure it was wise for Davy to go home, although I'd suggested it. Who could tell what he'd ingested in the past twenty-four hours? Perhaps he should go to the hospital, as a precaution. I dread decisions like these too. I'll take them for Marcie, just as she takes them for me. But other people ought to take their own decisions: that's how I look at things. Sometimes I don't feel comfortable with that, and then I get confused.

'Davy, old friend,' I said. 'You've spent the day on the booze and the pills. You've banged your head on the floor. I can't serve you another drink.'

Davy considered this refusal for a moment. 'On

second thoughts,' he said, 'I'll go home.' He took the car keys from his pocket. Marcie looked at me, hands firmly on hips.

'I'll take you back,' I said.

'There's no need for that.'

'Yes, there is. I'm taking you.'

I was still expecting an argument, but it didn't come. Davy resisted each suggestion once, as a reflex response, then submitted to it. I put an arm around his shoulder and we wove our way through the swing doors and into the parking lot. I slid him into my car and we set off. I knew roughly where he lived, but not exactly, which was as much as he knew at the time. Eventually we came to an apartment block a little way from the town centre and Davy decided this was the place. Having dropped the keys twice, he let me open the door for him.

I've been to the homes of a few of my regulars over the years, but not many. Sometimes, Marcie and I like to imagine the places where they live. It's rare to get the opportunity to see if we're right or not. In this case we were right in principle, but hadn't foreseen the scale of it. The place was a wreck. Food cartons and beer cans lying around; a couple of chairs on their backs; stains on the carpet. The place stank too, of old grease and sweat. It hadn't got that way in the space of a fortnight. I couldn't help noticing a smashed photo of Arlene in the corner. And one of another woman, not smashed.

'No place like home,' said Davy.

He surveyed the scene in silence, a long pan shot round the room and back again. My eyes tracked his and then met them.

'Did the two of you have a fight?'

'Nope.'

'Did you ever hit her?'

'Nope.'

'Are you sure?'

'Yup.'

'How did the place get like this?'

'I'm not the tidiest,' he said, 'and I chucked a few things around last night.'

'Can I use the bathroom?'

'Sure. It's through there.'

I didn't need to use the bathroom. I wanted to see it, and the bedroom too, if I could. Both were in a similar state to the sitting room.

'Want a beer?'

'No, thanks.'

Davy already had one and was popping a couple of pills.

'Take a seat,' he said. 'Make yourself at home.'

'I can't stay long. Can't leave Marcie and Steve alone on a Saturday night.'

'Don't see why not,' said Davy. 'Get on like a house on fire, those two.' He looked around his apartment. 'Go on. Say it.'

'Say what?'

'Tell me this place is a dump.'

'Did you bring Arlene here?'

'No.'

'Never?'

'No.'

'Where did you go?'

'To a motel.'

'Whose idea was that?'

'First off, it was Arlene's idea. I went along with it for . . .' Davy surveyed the room again. '. . . for obvious reasons. Then it became a habit. It gave us an equality. I didn't know where she lived, and she didn't know where I lived. It made us feel we were two strangers, meeting for the first time in a cheap motel, having an illicit affair. We liked that idea. It turned us on.'

'Which motel did you use?'

'The Albany Lodge,' said Davy. Not the answer I was expecting.

'Where did Arlene go in the mornings?'

'She didn't wait till morning. She left in the night.'

'Always?'

'Always. I did too. When she'd gone, I got dressed and came back here.'

'Where did you think it was going?' I asked. Davy looked at his beer can and said nothing. 'Did you think it was going anywhere?'

After a long silence, Davy answered. 'I don't think anything's going anywhere,' he said.

'What does that mean?'

'I'm not sure what it means. I think what it means is that I've been treading water for the last two years. Maybe that's all I'll ever do now.'

To listen to him, you wouldn't think that Davy was dosed up with booze and tranquillizers. He was more lucid than most sober men. However, I didn't feel his presence in the room. He was someplace else, with me peering through the window, trying to discern where that place might be. His voice acknowledged my presence; his eyes did not. They were fixed on a point where two walls met the ceiling, three planes colliding in cracks to the plasterwork. Much the same as Arlene had done on the bench at Coney Island, only her horizon was wide and distant, and Davy's was close to home, or to where home had once been.

'I should be getting back,' I said. 'Do you reckon you'll be all right on your own tonight?'

'I guess so.' His eyes were fixed on the cracks.

'I'll be seeing you then.'

That wasn't the end of this story. Two weeks later, in mid-July, Arlene came back. Doors swung open, and an orange coat, black purse, lipstick and attitude slunk in. She waltzed up to Steve at the counter, ordered a vodka Martini and asked if Davy was around. Within a week, the two of them were back together.

Horses with three legs sometimes win races, I suppose, if the other runners forget to pitch up. The odds of this reunion happening were on a par with that. It was the first time we'd seen Arlene since the split, although we'd seen plenty of Davy. We'd also seen plenty of Franky. The two of them, Davy and Franky, had spent a few long evenings talking in a corner of the bar. Since Marcie and I suspected Franky of having designs on Arlene, and the other way about, and since we had surmised that the two of them might already be an item, this was strange to say the least. We debated whether to warn Davy. As usual, we decided we wouldn't. We knew nothing for certain. Experience said that poking our noses into the affairs of our customers was never a good idea.

We got the impression that Franky was the prime mover in these conversations. This invited the usual question as to his motives. Davy seemed to have no suspicions on that score, but Davy didn't know Franky as well as we did. He told Marcie that Franky had been a real help in getting him over Arlene. He told her he found Franky easy to talk to, which was true enough. He said that Franky was one of the few people to take an interest in his life. That was surely untrue. Davy believed it.

I remain perplexed by the episode. In many ways, I am more perplexed by it than by anything else in this story. It doesn't make sense to me. Most of the time, you take educated guesses about situations, and the guesses prove educated enough to have got a college degree. Not this time. Marcie and I never understood the two-way flow between Davy and Franky. Nor the three-way flow when Arlene joined in. I suppose, sometimes, you have to accept that there are things that you don't know, that you don't understand, and that you'll never figure out. Whatever lay behind it, Arlene and Davy were back together.

It was different this time around. In any relationship, there's someone who kisses and someone who allows themselves to be kissed. That's not original. Someone else said it first. I don't know who. A Frenchman, from the sound of it.

At the beginning, Arlene allowed herself to be kissed. Others disagree with that statement. They think that no one with so much attitude allows things to happen to them. I think they're wrong. They're wrong in the way that men are frequently wrong, if I may slander my gender. They think it's to do with sex. Sometimes it is to do with sex, often maybe, but not always. Men think that attractive women like Arlene, who make the most of themselves, must be up for it. That's one mistake. They also assume that the plain and mousy ones aren't up for it. That's another mistake.

I don't think Arlene was much interested in sex. That's my opinion. No one agrees with me on that, not even Marcie. I think Arlene accepted that sex was something that happened from time to time, like a winter cold or a bee sting, so there wasn't much point complaining, as long as it didn't happen too often. That suggests that Arlene must have been interested in love. I don't believe that either. She didn't think it existed, is my guess.

The first time around, it was Davy who had done the kissing and Arlene who'd allowed herself to be kissed. The second time around it was the opposite. It was Arlene who did the coming back, Arlene who sought out Davy, and Arlene who suggested they got back together. Aha, people said, why would she do that if she didn't want sex or love or both?

Because she was lonely, if you ask me. That's at the heart of this. Arlene was lonely, forever lonely, desperately lonely. Loneliness filled her being. She came to the bar because she wanted companionship. She may have been looking for Jack, but that's not a full-time occupation, and she must have known by now she wouldn't find him here. She split up with Davy because he wasn't making her happy. She came back to him because splitting up had reminded her she was lonely.

Perhaps she did go to Indiana, and hadn't expected to come back.

Still doesn't explain why she didn't take up with Franky at that point. Maybe he wasn't ready for her yet. Of course, she might already have taken up with Franky. If so, they both kept it well hid.

7

'A rock star,' said Mike. 'What did you want to be?'

'A professor,' I said.

'The President,' said Nelson.

'Beggar man, thief,' said Steve. Marcie cuffed him gently on the head. 'Just kidding,' he said.

'Myself,' said Marcie. We looked at Franky.

'Somebody,' he said.

'Looks like I'm the only one who made it,' said Marcie.

'Not so difficult if you aim low.' That was Franky speaking. He was in one of his truculent moods. 'Besides, there's a distance to go. You'll know all about me one day. The train hasn't called at my platform yet.'

'That's because it doesn't stop there,' said Marcie.

'I'll derail the bastard then.'

'Then you won't be going anywhere,' said Marcie. 'Just like now.' Mike laughed.

'What are you laughing at, you jerk?' said Franky. 'What do you know about anything? Wanted to be a rock star and ended up a bank clerk.'

'The story of our time,' said Mike.

'You can't blame anyone for not winning the lottery,' said Nelson. 'Which is what it amounts to, if you ask me. I go on buying the tickets.'

'Yeah, OK,' said Franky. 'I get frustrated, that's all. I don't like the odds. When Andy Warhol said everyone would have fifteen minutes of fame, that was bullshit. Fame isn't democratic. It's a lifetime of fame or nothing. I want to shift the odds. Of course, there are ways of shifting the odds that bring you a few minutes of fame straight off.'

'Like what?' asked Mike.

'Like if I happened to have a gun on me,' said Franky. He put his hand in his coat pocket. 'And if I happened to point it at Marcie.' He raised his fingers toward her through the coat. 'And if it happened to go bang bang. Then I'd be famous, right? I'd be on the local news. In fact, I'd be on the national news.'

'Don't flatter yourself,' said Marcie, cool as you like, hands on hips. The rest of us stared, mouths open.

'Just saying,' said Franky. 'Hey, lighten up, you lot.' When that didn't improve the atmosphere, he drained his glass and headed for the door. 'See you around, guys.'

'What the hell was that about?' asked Mike.

Ever since Franky had come back to town, whenever he and Marcie had been in the same room, there'd been this sizzle between them. I don't mean a romantic sizzle: if anything, it was the opposite. I mean an electric surge of the sort that might fry you if you weren't careful. Marcie and I had discussed Franky from time to time during the years he'd been absent. We never said anything different, but we said it often, because he was the sort of guy who refused to be forgotten. So I knew that Marcie didn't trust Franky and she didn't like him. And Marcie knew that I didn't trust Franky either, but that I did like him. She could never figure that out. I stick by it. If all my friends wore halos, I'd be bored as hell.

Since Franky's return, there'd been this charge between them. Marcie was good at putting people down. It was a skill she used sparingly and only with people she didn't like. Her put-downs of Franky had been venomous at times. Remarks she might have made to others with half a laugh were made to him unsmilingly. And Franky's response had been defensive every time, which was peculiar, because Franky and defensiveness didn't go together. Until now, that is, when it had become aggressive. This made me more convinced that Marcie had some hold over him. I'd wanted to ask her, yet I hadn't. I don't think I wanted to know the answer. Now Marcie supplied it herself, or appeared to.

'I'll tell you what it was about, Mike. Franky thinks I know something that he doesn't want anyone else to know.'

'Like what?'

'Search me. I know nothing that several dozen other people in town don't know. But Franky thinks I do.'

'Have the two of you discussed it since he came back?' I asked.

'Sure. Franky talked to me soon after he arrived. He said he'd appreciate it if I didn't mention what I knew. I said I didn't know anything. The more times I said that, the more Franky was convinced I must know. So we play this game.'

'Threatening to shoot you isn't a game,' said Mike.

'He wasn't threatening that,' said Marcie. 'And it is a game, although Franky's serious about not wanting something to be known. He's a coward, anyhow. If it's only a crime that will bring him fame, it won't be murder, you can be sure of that.'

I wished I could be sure of it. I wished I could be sure of anything where Franky was concerned. I felt uncomfortable with the way Marcie behaved toward Franky. It had the authenticity of a melodrama. Look at me, she seemed to be saying, see how I taunt him, see how I despise him. It's a well-known fact that opposites attract. Like most well-known facts, it's not a fact at all, but it's sometimes true and I'd been wondering for a while if it was true with Marcie and Franky. Both ways round. If Franky thought Marcie had information he didn't want publicized, you'd think he wouldn't spend much time hanging out in our bar. So why did he? And Marcie was definitely spending fewer evenings watching TV these days.

Marcie and I have no secrets from one another. We

tell that to each other constantly, so it must be true. Yet she'd never told me what she told the group in the bar that night, which you'd think she might have done the moment she'd had that first conversation with Franky. Assuming she did have it. I'm not saying I suspected the two of them of having an affair. The lives we led would have made that difficult, not to say impossible. However, I was darned sure there was more to the situation than they were letting on. I reckoned that Marcie's public explanation for Franky's threat was made, not because it was true, but because some explanation was required to put a stop to further debate.

From that evening, the thing was on my mind. It became a fixed idea with me that there was some history between them, some secret that was not shared with me. I had no notion what it was, but I didn't believe the explanation Marcie had given that evening. It became a challenge to find the true answer. As things turned out, this mystery had to give way to another mystery for a while. An old mystery that came back to haunt us.

As you drive west out of town, the bar is nearly the last building before you reach the crossroads where E. A. Stuart's bench used to stand. After that, you leave the limits. To be precise, the bar's the last building except for one. That one doesn't really count. It doesn't belong to the town, or doesn't seem to. It's a substantial house, not far short of mansion size, but it's as invisible as its occupant. The place is surrounded by trees, the ones Franky was climbing: not in the sense of a pleasant landscaping, but of a deliberate envelopment. The trees are tall and dark and evergreen, acting as a perimeter fence to the property. I was going to say like a prison wall, but prison walls are there to keep insiders in, and those trees were there to keep outsiders out.

I hadn't seen the house for thirty years or more, despite having lived next to it for half of them. When we were kids, we used to slip through the wire into the garden to take a look around. On one occasion we got right to the back door, but we'd triggered some form of alarm system, and had to run like hell when the klaxon sounded. Franky was with us on that occasion, if I remember rightly.

You couldn't see the house from the road. There were big iron gates, bolted but not padlocked. I hadn't seen a car go in or out for years but, if it happened seldom, there's no reason I would have done. Beyond the gates, the drive bent, hemmed in by laurel bushes, so the house was obscured. About the only view you could get of it, without entering the grounds, was from up one of the pine trees, as Franky must have figured.

We called it Mr Hammond's house because it was supposed to be occupied by a Mr Hammond. We had no proof because no one had ever seen him. He was said to be tended by a series of housekeepers. I don't know how many there had been over time – at least a dozen, I should think. They seemed to stay a few years, then move on. Whether Mr Hammond got dissatisfied with them, or whether they went gradually insane with their strange life, I couldn't say. People had seen them, because they went to the shops to buy things for the household. People had said 'good morning' to them and had usually got a 'good morning' back, though not accompanied by a smile or any small talk. It seemed unlikely that their employer had coincidentally acquired upwards of a dozen women whose vocabulary didn't extend beyond 'good morning'. This had to be a deliberate policy on Mr Hammond's part, we assumed.

I can't remember the last reported sighting of a housekeeper. Perhaps about five years ago, at a guess, but it could have been more or less. Doesn't mean they weren't still there, getting their groceries in some other town. Even if they weren't, Mr Hammond might still have been in the house himself. As a corpse, possibly.

There were a number of theories as to who this man was, and what his tale was. I was as fond as the next guy of encouraging them. I used to run a 'Mr Hammond Night' in the bar once a year, with a prize for the customer who made up the best account of his past. These stories got repeated around town, and sometimes I would be retold one a few years later by someone who swore it was the truth. The fact was we knew nothing except his name, and I now forget how we knew that, so perhaps someone had invented that too. We didn't know how old he was. He was already here when my parents came to town, soon before I was born, so he must have been a young man when he arrived, and he must have been an old man now, if he was still alive.

Which made his choice of life the more remarkable. I'm not the reclusive type myself, but I can see that a guy of around my age or older, who has made some money and had some bad experiences, might want to shut himself off from the world. I can't imagine why a young man should want to do that, or how it would be possible to live that way for so many years without going nuts. Perhaps Mr Hammond was nuts.

In the absence of facts, theories flourish. The 'Mr Hammond Nights' might have become a thing of the past, but that didn't stop us discussing him from time to time, and everyone had their point of view. There was no consensus, even on the fundamentals. Nelson used to pronounce as a certainty that Mr Hammond must be a multimillionaire. He said you couldn't live for decades, not working, without a big stash of dough behind you. Marcie didn't agree. She reckoned that, if Mr Hammond owned the house, which we didn't know, he could live the way he did without spending much at all, so – while he must have some money behind him – he might not have a lot. Nelson pointed out that the housekeepers wouldn't come cheap. Steve said that they could have been relatives. I thought no one could have that many female relatives prepared to spend a chunk of their lives that way. Mike said his grandfather had been the sibling of no fewer than ten sisters. Besides, Marcie said, we never took much notice of the housekeepers, so who was to say the eleventh hadn't also been the eighth, and perhaps the first and the fourth as well. She was right. When we each tried to describe the housekeepers, it turned out that no one could recall any of them clearly.

Toward the end of July, I decided it was time to revive the 'Mr Hammond Nights'. Perhaps I was subconsciously influenced by Franky's adventure up the tree. I announced one for the last Monday of the month. It was the beginning of vacation time. People were going away; the bar was getting emptier in the evenings, and we were in need of a distraction. Nothing much happened on Monday evenings at the best of times. The regulars said they'd be there. That included Davy and Arlene, now back together. It was Steve's night off. We forsook the bar area, me and Marcie included, and I put four tables together down the far end of the long bar room. There were twelve of us, as I recall, including some of the semi-regulars. I stood the first round of drinks, as had become the tradition, then everyone else pitched in. Quite a lot was drunk that night. Even Arlene bought a round.

A few years earlier, I'd acquired the head and shoulders of a mannequin from an outfitter's that was closing down. Marcie had embellished it with a pair of sunglasses, a trilby hat, tipped down over the eyes, and a muffler, wrapped round the neck and mouth. It looked as much alive as Howard Hughes. Maybe more so. The mannequin was passed solemnly round the table, anti-clockwise. The deal was that everyone had to speak in turn and relate Mr Hammond's backstory. No exceptions. If a stranger came in for a beer, he'd have to join in too. In fact, there was one exception. In other years, it had been Marcie: she fetched the drinks and acted as judge. This year, she decided to take part. I became judge and barman, which was as well because I was short on imagination for inventing new stories. We drew lots for the order of ceremonies and Davy went first.

'Hammond H. Hammond,' he began.

'Wait a minute,' said Nelson. 'What's the middle H. for?'

'Hammond.'

'So he's Hammond Hammond Hammond?'

'Yes,' said Davy. 'His grandfather was Hammond. His father was Hammond Hammond. He's Hammond Hammond Hammond. He shortened it to Hammond H. Hammond for convenience.'

'I pity his great-grandson,' said Marcie.

'He won't have one. He doesn't have kids. Will you let me tell my story, please?'

'OK,' I said. 'Get on with it.'

'Hammond the first was a religious entrepreneur,' said Davy. 'He built up a chain of churches in Arizona, then diversified into an evangelical TV station in Phoenix. His son merged it with another religion, then sold it to a gambling syndicate that was looking to expand.

120

Hammond H. Hammond is a recluse who lives off the proceeds.'

'What does he believe?'

'Nothing. He's an atheist. His grandfather's core belief was that money was sacred.'

'No wonder he did so well,' said Marcie.

'The women we see in town,' said Davy, 'indeed act as his housekeepers, but they're acolytes of his grand-pop's religion. They worship H^3, as he's affectionately known.'

'I think I'm going to found a religion,' said Arlene. 'Why were all religions set up by men? It's about time a woman started one.'

'I'll be there every Sunday,' said Franky, 'kneeling in front of you.'

'Your turn, dearest,' I said.

'The man's name was Douglas Hammond,' said Marcie. 'He owned a farm machinery company that sold equipment to businesses across the Midwest. He made a fortune. He was a bigamist. By the end of his life, he had three wives and a house for each of them in a different town. That's why we didn't see him. When he'd had enough of the wives, he came here. He didn't have a wife in this house. The women were his secretaries, or so he claimed. In fact, they were hookers, sent here to keep their hand in, or whatever. He died three years ago, in a brothel in Akron.'

'Who owns the house next door now?' asked Arlene.

'No one. It's empty. Has been for ages. Hammond didn't use it for the last years of his life.'

'Good try,' I said. 'But I saw someone there the other day.'

'Did you?' said Marcie. She seemed surprised. 'Who?'

'I don't know. I was peering through the shrubbery and it was a long way away. It looked like a woman. A housekeeper, I assumed.'

'As I mentioned, they weren't housekeepers,' said Marcie. 'One of the whores came back once or twice after he died, not recently. That's not to say that strangers mightn't have been nosing around the place. Mightn't they, Franky?'

Franky said nothing.

'It's your turn, Franky,' I said. 'What's your take on Mr Hammond?'

'Well,' he said. 'I know a great deal more than the rest of you. Mr Hammond was a friend of my mom and dad. When I was a kid, I saw him quite often. He was real good to me. Used to bring me presents and stuff.'

We were electrified.

'You never told us that,' I said.

'I haven't been around to tell you,' said Franky. 'Anyway, years ago, when I hadn't seen him for a while, I asked my mom what had happened to him.'

'What did she say?'

'She said he was ill and was confined to bed. Apparently he used to work for a pharmaceutical company.

Earlier, he'd been their sales manager in some country in Africa, where he contracted this incurable disease. He didn't know he had it for a while. The bug lay dormant for years. Then he got taken ill. His company bought the house next door for him to live in, and hired a nurse to care for him. From what you've said, there were several of them over time. As long as no one touched him, it seemed to be OK. He's dead now. At least, I imagine he is. I presume the house is empty.'

'Very good,' I said. 'Now would you care to tell us which parts of that story are true, if any, and which are made up.'

'From what you said at the beginning, those aren't the rules of the game. We tell our stories and you decide which one's the winner. Isn't that right?'

There was silence round the table. Arlene dabbed her eyes with a handkerchief.

'Why are you crying?' asked Marcie.

'I was thinking of that poor man and his illness,' said Arlene.

It's amazing what bullshit can achieve.

No one said a word. If I'd been asked to vote that second, I expect I would have voted for Franky's story. That didn't make it true. Franky's career had been founded on inventing stories that people believed. The other stories weren't true either. Unless someone had been smitten by a flash of intuition and had got close to the truth by accident.

I can't remember the detail of the other stories that night, except for Arlene's, which came at the end. There was the usual quota of aliens and spies. We had a retired mobster from Chicago with the real name of Giuseppe Amendola. Someone, Mike I think, said that Mr Hammond suffered from a rare condition called . . . I can't remember what it's called. It means fear of the daylight. Someone tried to persuade us that we had Elvis for a neighbour. We played 'Blue Suede Shoes' full blast on the jukebox, and opened the doors so we could hear if he came out to duet with himself. He didn't.

'OK,' said Franky to Arlene. 'You're the last to go. Beat my story.'

'It's not complicated,' said Arlene. 'It doesn't involve weird religions, multiple wives or incurable diseases. Mr Hammond doesn't exist. He never has. Nor have his housekeepers. The women themselves have existed, I suppose, but no one has asked them who they are, so no one knows. When the storekeepers in town see a woman they don't recognize, they assume it's Mr Hammond's latest housekeeper. They keep the myth alive. Everything has been assumed. Everything has been guesswork. It's all gossip, built up over the years. There's an empty house. Big deal. The country's full of empty houses. No one lives in it, or has done in living memory. So no Mr Hammond. No housekeepers. No nothing.'

I declared Arlene the winner of the competition. In the many debates about Mr Hammond over the years, I don't think it had occurred to us that he might not exist, and that no one lived in that house, or ever had done.

Afterwards, Marcie went to bed and everyone else went home. Except for Franky and Davy. When I'd cleared away, they were sitting at the bar, deep in conversation.

'Davy thinks the two of us should go over to Mr Hammond's house one day and take a look around,' said Franky.

'It was you that suggested that, Franky.' Davy looked at me. 'Want to come with us?'

'You mean, take a look around the garden?'

'Yeah, and perhaps the house as well,' said Franky. 'Depends what we find. What do you think?'

The first thing I thought was that it was trespass. I've got more law-abiding these days. The second thing was that I was curious. The third thing was that Franky and Davy were going to do it whatever I said, so I might as well join them.

'I'm in,' I said.

I was happy to be in on something for once. I was beginning to feel left out of whatever was going on around me.

8

Once he'd got the idea into his head, Franky didn't waste time. He and Davy came round the next Saturday morning and off we went through our parking lot to Mr Hammond's place. We could have gone in by the main gates, but didn't want to run the risk of being noticed. I provided the wire cutters and clipped the fence. Franky took the lead. 'You shouldn't have let him do that,' Marcie said afterwards; 'it's not his town now; you're not kids anymore.' It was nothing to do with being kids or not being kids. Some things don't change.

I cut the wire with care, enough to let us in without wanton destruction. After the wire came the undergrowth, thickets of brambles and shrubs, and within the thickets were the trunks of pine trees. We walked on a carpet of needles, knees raised high to avoid entanglement, like we were playing Grandma's Footsteps. It took several minutes till we got through into what had once been the garden; until we got our view of the house.

'Jesus Christ,' said Davy.

When Franky and I had done this as kids, there had

been a lawn, of sorts. Now there was no lawn, just thick, long grass, full of weeds that had tumbled under their own weight like matted dreadlocks. Then the house had looked, well, I wouldn't say cared for, but not entirely uncared for. Unkempt; not dilapidated. Now the paint-work peeled, a window hung off its hinges, and dark green stains ran down the walls where clogged and broken guttering had diverted the rainwaters from their course.

'Jesus Christ,' said Davy again.

'Arlene was right,' said Franky. 'No one living here now.'

'How long has it been empty, do you reckon?' I asked.

'Can't be less than five years, I'd think,' said Davy. Was that right? How long did it take for cobwebs to spread, for floorboards to creak, for windows to leak? How long did it take for life to seep out of a house?

We looked at each other and pressed on. I don't know what the others were thinking. To me it felt an intrusion, like treading on ground where a sadness had been buried. It didn't feel that we had a right to be there. Of course, we didn't have a right to be there, but now we'd come we weren't going back. I didn't want to be there, and I didn't want to leave.

Franky picked his way toward the back door, like we'd done thirty years earlier, although there was now no reason not to try the front. The door was not locked. In fact, it was slightly ajar. It creaked on its hinges as

Franky pushed it open, me and Davy close behind him. I hadn't thought to bring a flashlight. I hadn't imagined we'd really go inside the house. We were going to take a look around, I thought, to see what was going on, in a general kind of way. I hadn't guessed that nothing was going on.

Franky took a hesitating step down what seemed to be a corridor, the doors that led from it securely closed. We were in darkness. If I'd been on my own, I would have skedaddled at this point. I'm a scaredy-cat when it comes to situations like this. Franky wasn't a scaredy-cat, and neither was Davy. They weren't for going. Franky paused for a while, letting his eyes acclimatize to the darkness, then turned a handle and pushed open a door. He fiddled for a light switch and found it. No light came on.

There were shutters on the window. They didn't fit too well and a shard of light lay on the floor from the gap between them. Enough light to see that the room was empty. Enough light for Franky to reach the window and open the shutters. The three of us stood there and looked around and said nothing. It was a warm, bright day outside. Inside, it felt cold. The warm air chilled as it percolated through the window and circulated round the room. It felt like the first air the room had known in years. Dust lay thick on the surfaces and swirled like confetti in the sunbeams coming through the window. A moth with damaged wings stirred on the windowsill. The extremity of the silence screamed at us. Franky looked at his footprints on the floorboards. There was a set of smaller footprints next to them.

'I told you I saw someone here,' I said.

'Let's look upstairs,' said Franky.

I wasn't keen to go upstairs. I let the others move a few paces ahead of me, so they could discover whatever nastiness there was. It seemed to me that most things were possible. At any turn we might find a skeleton or, worse, a body in the act of decomposing. Not that decomposing is an act, I suppose. It's a process: a stage in the journey from something to nothing. Perhaps a protracted journey in this environment. Franky and Davy had no such qualms. They flung open doors and marched up staircases, unconcerned with what they might find. The other rooms were barren, like the first, except that upstairs there were no footprints. The only inhabitants of the house were dust and silence and a multitude of specimens from the insect kingdom. The place had been picked clean.

'Who told you that Mr Hammond lived here?' asked Davy. 'Or that anyone did?'

Franky and I looked at each other. 'I don't know,' I said. 'It was something we knew. Everybody knew it.'

'Did your parents tell you? Someone must have told you.'

'I don't know,' I said. 'When you've known a fact for forty-odd years, you don't question how you know it.'

'You didn't know it,' said Davy. 'Because it was wrong.'

'It was right once,' Franky said. He paused. 'According to my parents.'

'What about the housekeeper?' I said to Davy. 'And the other housekeepers? We haven't invented them.' I was keen to hang on to something concrete, something that could not be dematerialized so easily.

'How do you know they lived here? How do you know they kept house for Mr Hammond, or for anyone? How do you know there was a Mr Hammond?' I hadn't figured Davy for a state prosecutor. He could have made a decent job of it.

Good questions. How did we know? All I could say was that, at some point, we must have known, because facts like that don't simply get invented. Some certain knowledge had started it off, and we couldn't now remember what it was. There was no denying that the house was unoccupied, and looked as though it had been that way for several years. Someone must once have lived here and they must have moved out or died, and they, or someone else, must have cleared the place of furniture and belongings, must have pulled the doors and shutters closed behind them. And the second set of footsteps said that someone had been back since, and recently.

There were other questions too. Who owned the

house now? Did they know they owned it? Who would deliberately leave a valuable piece of real estate for this length of time, letting it crumble to pieces?

That evening in the bar, minus Franky, but aided by contributions from the female side of the brain in the shape of Marcie and Arlene, we laid the pieces on the counter and tried to put the puzzle together. Couldn't be done. Too many pieces missing. If Franky had partly been telling the truth on 'Mr Hammond Night', then there had indeed been a family connection between Hammond and the Albertinos, as Marcie had half remembered. I hoped that she would now pluck a further clue from her childhood memory that would make sense of everything. She couldn't do that, and said she was as mystified as the rest of us. She thought the clue was there, though, lodged somewhere beyond her reach. Arlene wasn't able to be of historical assistance, but she had a quirky mind and I thought she might find another way of looking at the puzzle that had escaped us.

'I gave you the answer the other night,' said Arlene. 'There's no Mr Hammond. No housekeepers. No one lives there.'

'That was a game,' said Davy.

'Not to me, it wasn't. I was being serious. I won the competition, remember?'

'Someone must have lived there once,' I said.

'Not necessarily,' said Arlene. 'Someone bought the

land, had the house built, died before they could occupy it. Why not? Can't have been the first time it's happened.'

'When we went there years ago,' I said, 'there was a klaxon to warn us off.'

'So? An alarm system was fitted when the house was built.'

'This isn't getting us anywhere,' I said. 'What's the point?'

'The point,' said Arlene, 'is that if you don't know for certain what happened, anything could have happened. You can make up what you like and it's as possible as anything else. Anyone can choose to believe it or not to believe it. That's the point.'

'You were right,' said Marcie, looking at Arlene. 'You should start a religion.'

On the Monday, Marcie and I chewed over what we'd learned. Once upon a time, there may have been a genuine Mr Hammond and a genuine housekeeper who looked after him. Several millennia ago, back when Noah was parking his ark on Mount Ararat. Since then it had been assumptions.

'Where would the world be if we all carried on that way?' I asked Marcie.

'Same place as it is,' she said.

'It has occurred to me,' I said, 'that the second set of footprints in the house might have belonged to Arlene.'

'Why should they?'

'She wasn't far off on "Mr Hammond Night", with the idea of an abandoned property. Maybe she'd been there.'

'I don't know,' said Marcie. 'It's not that far-fetched an idea that the place might be empty. If Arlene knew something about the house that no one else knew, everything we've learned of Arlene says she'd have kept it to herself.'

'Maybe Arlene has some connection with the house, and that's what she's keeping secret.'

'Arlene's been around for nearly six months,' said Marcie. 'She hasn't shown any interest in the house. Franky's the one who's done that.'

'We've no idea what Arlene's interested in beyond Jack. We don't know she's not interested in the house, or that she hasn't been there.'

That might have been the end of the debate, but it wasn't. A day or two later, Franky approached me in the bar and asked if he could have a word. Sure, I said. A quiet word, he said, motioning with his head to the corner. Franky and I took our drinks to a vacant table.

'I've been thinking,' said Franky.

'Yeah?'

'I like it here. Feels like I've come home. I wouldn't mind staying. However, there's a slight problem. Fact is, I haven't got too much money.' Uh-oh, I thought, here comes the sting. I'd been expecting it for weeks.

'What I was thinking,' said Franky, 'was here's this

house, right next door to you, that doesn't seem to belong to anybody. With a bit of attention and a lick of paint, it would make a real nice home. It's a shame to see it go to waste like this. I'd be doing someone a favour.'

'You want to squat there?'

'I wouldn't put it that way,' said Franky. 'I'd be renovating the place, doing it up. I'd be more like some kind of caretaker.'

'And if the owner showed up?'

'I'd move out. And the owner would be glad to have a smart property at no expense. Winners all round, so long as it doesn't happen anytime soon. If you ask me, it isn't going to happen at all. In time, I dare say I'll become the legal owner.'

'How's that?'

'Possession's nine tenths of the law, so I've been told.'

'I don't think that applies to real estate, Franky.'

'It did when we were building this country. It was ten tenths then.'

'What about electricity and water?' I asked.

'Yes. That could be a problem,' said Franky. 'Not the water. I tried two of the taps when we were there and the water's still on, for some reason. I'm not sure if the drainage works. That might be a problem. And the electricity's definitely a problem. Perhaps I could get a generator. I've got another idea, though.'

'What is it, Franky?'

'I've worked in the electricity business. Know a lot about it. On the technical side.'

'So?'

'This place of yours is the next property. If you could tell me where your electricity supply comes in, I think I could divert some of it next door. I mean, before it gets to your meter. It wouldn't cost you anything.'

'That would be illegal, Franky.'

'Possibly. Technically speaking.'

'Definitely. You can't go round stealing electricity.'

'My risk,' said Franky. 'You wouldn't need to know. Officially.'

'Why are you telling me, if I don't need to know?'

'It's a neighbourly thing to do,' said Franky. In his mind, he was already our neighbour.

I don't think that was why he told me. If this was what he wanted to do, he could have gone right ahead and done it. The electricity supply was a long way outside, and I bet he knew that. He could have tampered with it without my knowledge. I think he wanted Marcie's approval for the scheme. He knew that if he told me, I would tell Marcie. Approval is too strong a word. Marcie was never going to approve such a scheme, or any scheme that Franky proposed. What he wanted was Marcie's acquiescence. He didn't want her going round town bad-mouthing him for what he was doing. She didn't have to be positive. She could say nothing. That would do fine.

'You shouldn't have told me, Franky,' I said. 'The answer's no. I can't possibly agree to that.'

'I'll have to find another way round the problem then. I'm moving in and that's for certain.'

I related this conversation to Marcie later that evening.

'Now we know why he wanted to look next door,' she said.

'He said it was Davy's idea. Davy said it was Franky's idea.'

'Who would you believe?'

'Fair enough,' I said.

'I told you no good would come of it.'

'Come of what?'

'Of Franky being back in town. Trouble's his middle name. In fact, it's all his names. He's Trouble T. Trouble.'

'He's got a point, though,' I said. 'Now we know there's no Mr Hammond, and no one living there, and no one who's lived there for years. You should have seen the place, Marcie. Give it a little more time and it'll start falling down. What good would that do anyone? If Franky does it up like he says, that's good news for everyone. As long as he gets out if the owner comes back to claim it. That's all right, isn't it?'

'It would be fine,' said Marcie, 'if it was anyone else. Not when it's Franky Albertino. Something will go wrong.'

'I think he needs your acceptance of it.'

'If it pours down with rain, I accept it,' said Marcie. 'Doesn't mean I like it. Franky should never have come back. Some people should never come back. Most people, in fact. It's a bad idea.'

'You must admit he hasn't done anything wrong yet,' I said.

'Stealing electricity's not wrong suddenly?'

'Apart from that.'

'If I pinned the Ten Commandments on the wall to remind him what they are, he'd break each of them given time.'

Time was the one thing it seemed we would have. Franky pushed ahead with his scheme. He discovered that there were dormant utility accounts in the name of Hammond, so he hit on the idea of changing his name. He was now Franky Hammond, officially. I don't know how he managed to swing that one. You're meant to have a good legal reason to change your name. Franky said his lawyer fixed it. So he had a lawyer now.

He gave the house a makeover, and he gave himself a makeover. He even announced that he'd got a job. What made me uncomfortable, and Marcie too, was that he appeared not to have told anyone except us what he was doing next door, or that he'd changed his name. When he was in the bar, he didn't mention the house, except to us, and in a whisper. He had drawn us into a conspiracy without our having had a say in the matter. He didn't tell us it was a secret, but we felt obligated to treat it as one.

We don't like secrets. Besides, if you're running a bar and you've got several regulars you've known for years and discussed everything with, they'd feel put out if you withheld crucial information from them. Worse, it would make them think, when they found out, which they would, that we'd been cut in on a deal, that we'd been underhand. We didn't see why we should be put in that position with friends who'd been good to us for years, least of all by Franky, who'd stitched the town up as a kid and had been gone for more than a quarter-century.

One night, when it wasn't too busy and we could leave Steve minding the bar, we took him to a quiet table and had it out with him.

'This place you're working, Franky,' I said. 'I imagine they asked for your address. What did you tell them?'

'I'm not actually working,' said Franky. 'Not at present.'

'You told me you'd got a job.'

'I was a little ahead of myself. I've signed on with an employment agency. I'm sure they'll find me a position soon.' Marcie raised both eyebrows, one after the other, and put both hands on her hips. Triple somersault with pike.

'All right,' I said. 'So what address did you give when the employment agency asked?'

'Care of you,' said Franky. 'I hope you don't mind.'

Marcie exploded a breath at him and looked at me to continue the prosecution.

'We can't go on this way,' I said.

'What way?'

'With you and Marcie and me being the only ones to know what you're doing.'

'Why not?'

'Because we don't like it. Besides, you won't be able to keep it quiet. People will find out. It's a stupid thing to be doing. Much better to be upfront.'

'I don't see why people should find out,' said Franky. 'No one here seems to remember seeing the previous Mr Hammond.'

'That's because he didn't exist.' I'd started believing it myself now.

Franky looked at me. 'I'd rather you didn't tell anyone,' he said. 'Not for the moment. Later, perhaps, when I've kitted the place out and settled in properly.'

'Too late,' said Marcie. 'I've already told Arlene.'

Franky looked shocked. So did I, for that matter.

'Why did you do that?'

'Why shouldn't I do that? You didn't ask me not to.'

'Don't tell anyone else.' Franky decided this might sound a little abrupt. 'Please,' he added.

'Franky, this isn't going to work. Arlene will have told Davy, so he'll know.'

'No. He doesn't,' said Franky. 'Davy doesn't know.'

'Well, even if he doesn't, I'll be sort of bound to tell him, seeing as it was the three of us that went over the place. Other people will know too. Steve's probably wondering what the hell we're talking about right now. It's no longer a secret.'

Franky went off to the restroom.

'Did you really tell Arlene?' I asked Marcie.

'No,' said Marcie. 'But it upset him, didn't it?'

It did upset him, and I'm not sure if it was the fact of Marcie saying she'd told someone, or of her saying she'd told Arlene in particular.

'I've been thinking,' said Franky, when he returned. 'You were right, Marcie. Stupid of me to get so uptight.' Marcie and I glanced at each other. 'All the same, would you do me the courtesy of not mentioning it to anyone else for the time being? And also, to make it above board, I think I should be paying some kind of rent for the place.'

'Who are you proposing to pay it to?' asked Marcie.

'Why don't I pay it to you? You could look after it in case the owner returns.'

'We'll have a think about it,' I said.

Think about it, hell. We were being offered a bribe. Strings would come with the cash Franky gave us, or more likely the cash that Franky decided he owed us and might give us sometime later if we were lucky. We had no idea what the strings were attached to. Not our problem, you might say: we would just say no. But we'd still got pulled into the project. We were accomplices whether we liked it or not.

'There's another thing,' said Franky.

'Yes?'

'I'll need to get building materials and furniture delivered. And I'll need to leave my car somewhere while I'm at the house.'

'I believe it has a front drive,' said Marcie. 'That should suit your purpose.'

'I don't want to use it. I'll be seen. Questions will be asked. I told you. I don't want questions right now. Please can I use the space at the back of your house? No one can see it from the road. It would be perfect.'

Marcie gave me a threatening look. I knew what she meant, but saying no would be to declare war on Franky's project. I was reluctant to do that.

'There's no way through to the house from here,' I said.

'There is now. You cut the fence the other week.'

'What about the brambles and weeds?'

'I'll flatten them.'

I got another look from Marcie. We were on alien territory here. Usually, Marcie and I agreed with each other and, when we didn't, I usually gave way. Maybe I would have done now, if Marcie and I had been discussing it in private. I was loath to do it in front of Franky, who was also looking at me, waiting for a decision.

'You can do it for three months,' I said. 'And that's it.'

Franky proceeded to widen the hole I'd cut in the fence. He scythed the worst of the brambles and the grass and the weeds. He had a clear path to Mr Hammond's house. Unless someone came snooping round the back of our private quarters, his handiwork would be invisible to the outside world. We watched as building materials were delivered, and got used up. Franky wasn't wasting time. It was the beginning of August when he announced his plans. By mid-month his adopted house was a building site, as was the back of ours.

Marcie had been livid with my decision, and I couldn't fathom it myself. Why had I gone out on a limb for someone wielding a chainsaw?

'How do you suppose he's financing this?' she asked one day. 'He's here all the time.'

'We don't know he hasn't got money,' I said. 'We've assumed it. Maybe he's made his fortune and has come back here to spend it.'

'He doesn't have money. He told you that himself.'

'He may not have been telling the truth. He was trying to get my sympathy at the time.'

'If Franky had made his fortune,' said Marcie, 'he'd have been waving dollar bills in our faces the moment he got here.'

'At least he hasn't asked us for a loan.'

'Even Franky wouldn't have the nerve to do that. It doesn't mean he hasn't asked other people. There's a new generation of suckers in town. Who knows who's got the job of Franky's banker? And you can bet, whoever it is, they won't know either.'

9

I had a puzzle book as a kid. One puzzle had two drawings, apparently the same, and the task was to list twenty things that were different between them. I used to stare at the drawings, and at first I couldn't see a darned thing that was different. Then I spotted one thing, then another, till I had fourteen or fifteen of the twenty. As I noticed each one, the difference – previously unapparent to me – became glaring. How could I not have noticed that the four bars on the gate had become five, that the little girl's shoelace had come undone?

That's what it was like last summer, the first and last summer of Arlene, with its gradual revelations. Mostly, I feel that I've run like quicksilver through my years, but for those few months it was different. For a time, life was subtle, willing to share its innuendos with me. The longer I live, the more it seems that I've forgotten how to be subtle. We're not living in a subtle age, I suppose. We deal in bright sunlight or abject darkness. There's no shade, no shadow, no ambiguity. Everything is what it appears to be. It isn't, as we know.

It was past the midpoint of August. Next door, Franky was building his dream, or rebuilding someone else's. I watched from the sitting-room window as Marcie picked the flowers. The weather was grey and still, as it always seems to be on this day, even when it isn't. We don't have much of a garden and too little time to tend what we do have. Some flowers blossom, and other flowers, wild flowers, grow in the patch of land that separates us from Mr Hammond's property. That day, I could see flax there, and black-eyed Susans. There were more than enough flowers for two small bouquets.

Marcie selected them with care. Each bloom would have a considered place in its vase. What had been so carelessly lost would be carefully recalled. The harvest took twenty minutes, and they were small bouquets. No flower was discarded, once picked. Each flower was precious. Sometimes it took a minute or two for Marcie to select the next one. Once or twice she looked toward the window where I was watching behind lace curtains. She couldn't see me, but she knew I was there, because I was always there on this day.

When the flowers had been assembled, Marcie returned to the house, to the kitchen. She trimmed them with a paring knife and arranged them in two vases that had been a wedding present from my Great-uncle Alvin, and which had now acquired this purpose and no other. I watched this process too. When it was complete, when each stalk occupied its proper place, Marcie placed the vases on the sideboard. Then she went to the cupboard and took out the photograph, the one that was present on this day and on no other, and placed that on the sideboard also. She stood in contemplation and I stood beside her, my arm around her.

We did not speak. There was nothing to say. There never had been anything to say. All words were inadequate. We who talked freely, without premeditation, at other times, did not talk at this time. Once, perhaps, one or other of us might have inclined our head, the trace element of an ill-remembered ritual. We no longer did that. The ritual was hollow and what it symbolized no longer existed for us. Many things did not exist.

Sometime in the next few weeks, I would say that I felt like a break and I'd go fishing for a while. Before that, Marcie would go to Colorado for a few days. That would be announced in a few days' time. The departures were assumed and would not be discussed. She would go, and I would go, separately and at separate times, and then it would be the fall, the leaves would turn to gold, and life would resume.

It was in Colorado that it happened. At summer camp in Colorado, fifteen years ago. They weren't meant to go to there; we had other plans for that vacation. Those plans fell through, and Roseanne and Bobby had friends who were going to the camp, and they begged to go too, and there were a couple of vacancies, so we said yes. What parent wouldn't say yes? It was an accident.

No one was to blame. No one was ever to blame in those days. Now, fingers would be pointing everywhere. Yes, the staff could have been more vigilant. Yes, the driver was going too fast. We all drove too fast. We decided then that we weren't going to steep our souls in vinegar. We accepted then that it was one of those things.

Still, I don't like August. It isn't the sun so much, or the warmth. Those are things I like, on their own, shorn of their trappings. Nor is it the dappled sunlight in the garden, or the gold in the grain, or the dark green velvet of the leaves on the trees. These also are things I like, on their own, shorn of their trappings.

I do not like any part of summer: the season that recreates our innocence before destroying it. The season that is the repository of each false promise made to mankind, the worm within the apple, the darkness at the heart of the candle's flame. I do not like summer anywhere, even in places that are made for summer. I do not like beaches and parasols and cotton candy. I do not like summer camps.

I do not like the roads in summer, or the fast cars that bestride them. I do not like the conspiracy between the car and the road. I do not like the promise they make: to take you somewhere, to lead you somewhere. The promise of a perfection that hauls you forward, mile by mile, tempting you toward a beacon that does not exist, a mirage in a miasma, tempting you toward non-existence. May the gods preserve us from the idea of perfection.

I am a placid man. Everybody says that. And Marcie is a placid woman, as far as a woman can ever be placid. We wallow in our placidity. We are admired for it. But beneath the flat metal of our road, there is a rage. A rage that simmers and bubbles and boils in the crust of our world. A rage that rails against the deceits of summer and its trail of broken dreams. Our road is strewn with dreams discarded. Sometimes one of us suggests making a change to our lives. The other always finds a reason not to make the change, and the one who made the suggestion is always relieved. We go through the motions of life.

So give me the winter instead. Give me the still days of November, settled in mists and remembrances. Give me the chill days of February. Give me branches bare of leaves, and birds emptied of song. Give me roads without their siren calls of immortality. Give me life as it is, not life as it is sold as being. Life is November, and it is February, and it is the times between. Life is the unassuming months.

There's a time to be born and a time to die, the good book says. I can't remember when the last time was for borning, a while ago now, but August last year seemed, once again, to be the time for dying, although it was the height of summer and the leaves were a goodly green on the trees.

Mr Maflin down at the hardware store dropped dead one Saturday night after putting bolts on the door, like he'd done many thousand times before, and did now for the last time. Mrs George, who'd been my teacher in kindergarten, slipped away soon after. I'd thought she was eighty when she taught me. Turned out she was eighty-one when she died. She lived a long time in that year.

Then there was Great-uncle Alvin, and he was a hundred. My mom and dad were dead. My grandma, Alvin's oldest sister, was long dead. Alvin went on and on. He had lived in a home, a little way out of town, for fifteen years or more. He was a small man, wiry and strong. As he'd got older, he'd gotten smaller and wirier still, so that by the end he was like a double-concentrate version of himself. A stock cube of Alvin.

I would visit him once a month or so. His body was a sack of bones by the end; he couldn't see and he couldn't hear, but his mind was clear. At least it was clear on most things. One or two sectors had gone awry, such as believing that Marcie was called Roseanne. He'd started calling her by that name a few years earlier. To begin with, we'd correct him, then we stopped. The corrections caused us more heartache than an acceptance of the error. We'd known just the one Roseanne. He started calling me by the wrong name too, but it wasn't Bobby. He called me Dexter. We didn't know anyone called Dexter, and nor did he, so far as we knew. Roseanne and Dexter. That's what we became.

As it happened, I'd seen Alvin the evening before he

died. He was his same old self, wanting to know the baseball scores. Because of his hearing, he had a special alarm clock to wake him in the mornings. Last thing before I left, I asked him what time he wanted it set for, like I always did.

'Don't bother, Dexter,' he said. 'Won't be needing it tomorrow.' He died that night.

We're here for three score years and ten and rising. You'd think that would be enough to work out what most of it's about. I've got some years to go yet, I hope. I don't know what any of it's about. I don't know if Alvin decided to die that night, or if an instinct told him he was going to die, or if he felt like having a lie-in the next morning. Can't ask him now. Neither can I ask him why he chose to die in August, and whether he delayed it a few days out of consideration for us, or whether these things were coincidences.

Marcie wasn't around when Alvin died. She was in Colorado. She rang me from there on the day it happened. I withheld the news from her. The time belonged to Bobby and Roseanne, and Alvin would have been a gatecrasher. If that sounds mean, I don't deny that he deserved a time of his own, but he'd need to wait for it. He could have a different time of his own choosing.

Alvin's funeral fell on the anniversary of the other one, sixteen years earlier. It was the first time I'd been to a funeral on that day since then. Although I suppose you could say there's been a funeral every year. This year it was a shared funeral. My thoughts were on the one I was missing, that I always missed.

I mind that it happened in summer. I've always minded that. When branches are bare, when twigs snap in two on tombstone streets and frozen leaves shatter beneath the footfall, death belongs. You can't complain when it comes calling, when it comes to claim its own. Golden days, with crops ripening in the field, and berries there for the picking: these things are the properties of life. They should have been ours, and theirs. We had the pawn ticket in our pocket. We were going to redeem the promise made of dreamland, with hallelujahs and hosannas. Illusion, illusion, it was all illusion. The dream was snatched, and every leafy summer road led nowhere. One step back. Two steps back. I've lost count.

What it did, I think, was to neuter us, Marcie and me. Something holds us back all the time. We crouch behind cut-outs of ourselves. We don't lay our feelings on the line. We take care. We are too aware of how quickly, how unexpectedly, life can unravel. We watch what has happened to others. We see roads that are dyed red with the blood and entrails of elk that have mistimed their leaps between the juggernauts, and we do not leap. We respect the juggernauts of this world. If required, we will worship them.

When we buried Roseanne and Bobby, we buried pieces of ourselves. It's the other reason Marcie goes to Colorado, in my opinion. She goes to mourn lost pieces of herself. And of me. Human tissue and body parts, scattered on roads I now fear to travel.

When Alvin was buried, I stayed on a while in the cemetery. There was a wake back at his granddaughter's place, but I held my own wake there. In a corner of the graveyard, a young boy was picking wild flowers. He'd been there throughout the ceremony, keeping a respectful distance. Now he approached, flax and black-eyed Susans in hand.

'Was that Mr Ballard you were burying?'

'Yes,' I said. 'Did you know him?'

'No. I heard my pa talking about him.'

'Pretty flowers,' I said.

'My pa tends the graveyard. I always pick flowers when there's a burial.'

'To put on the grave?'

'Yeah,' said the boy. 'I like to do that. Sometimes there's no one here except the minister. It's not right.'

'What's your name?'

'Dexter,' said the boy.

'Well, Dexter, why don't we go put those flowers on Mr Ballard's grave.'

10

'The fact is,' Nelson said, 'I could have been congressman for this district. That opportunity was open to me. I turned it down.'

'We know,' said Mike.

'You know?'

'You already told us.'

'A dozen times,' I said.

There were just the three of us in the bar that evening. It was a Monday night in late August, but that was still poor business. Marcie was on her way back from Denver. It was Steve's night off. I don't know where the other regulars were. There was no passing trade.

Nelson was not a man to be deterred from a repeat performance of his monologue, even when there were no audible shouts of 'encore'. So we began to get the story again.

Nelson's political career went back to his days at college, where he'd been the brightest star in the political firmament, according to Nelson. Before you start getting the idea that he was some big shot at Yale or Harvard, I should mention that this was a small Methodist institution near Seattle, where the political firmament was usually obliterated by cloud cover. After college, he moved somewhere close to here and started work as an administrator in a local housing project. Before long, he had risen like yeast in the Democrat hierarchy and, according to Nelson, was regarded as the big high flyer in the state. Ten years ago, the Democrat bosses allegedly approached him and asked him to run for Congress. Nelson nobly passed on the chance, claiming he could serve the community better in other ways. That's the gist of the story. The full version takes up to two hours to recite. I haven't got that sort of time to spare. Nor, frankly, the interest.

Bullshit, according to the alternative version of events propagated by Nelson's wife or, to be precise, his ex-wife. Stephanie lives in the town of thieving bastards next door, which makes her an unreliable witness. Marcie sees her from time to time, having known her since they were both kids. Marcie says that Stephanie says the story is true up to the point where Nelson was being pressed to accept the nomination. This seems alarming in its own right, if you ask me, because it means that the state Democrats couldn't find a better candidate than Nelson to run for this district, which makes you wonder what the others were like. Amongst them, a person I probably voted for, come to think of it.

As Nelson's candidature was about to be announced,

someone investigated the charity he was running at the time and discovered a shortfall in the accounts of a million bucks. Secret bank accounts in Nelson's name were found in strange places. Some private dick started digging into his life at the charity's behest, and the long and short of it was that Nelson was allegedly paying the rent on a flash apartment in another city, in which lived a semi-clothed nightclub singer who doubled up as chairwoman of the fringe organization that had pushed for Nelson to be the candidate. To be clear, I'm not saying that this actually happened. It's what the ex-wife said.

You couldn't make this up, I said to Marcie. I couldn't, said Marcie, but Stephanie might have done. By her own admission, she'd resigned as president of Nelson's fan club soon after she married him, so couldn't be regarded as impartial. Nelson wasn't prosecuted. According to Stephanie, the charity decided that a court case would be bad for business. So they made him pay the money back, and he quit his post a few months later with glowing testimonials, which enabled him to get a job running another charity, right here in town.

The story might be true, or it might not. I've no idea. Nobody else knows either, at least no one you can trust. So there are two different versions of Nelson. He's a philanthropist who sacrificed a political career for the sake of his principles, or he's a crook. Take your pick. Whichever it is, he's close to setting the world marathon record for boredom, and his chosen venue is my bar.

Gossip's got spicier since I was a kid, like the food we eat. I think that's because life has got more bland and we need to compensate. If I'd expressed the opinion to my parents that our congressman maintained a nightclub singer in an embezzled apartment, I'd have been sent to my room and told to rinse my mouth out. Congressmen didn't do that sort of thing. They had idyllic sex with their pristine wives, prior to going to the Capitol to pass immaculate legislation on our behalf. Congressmen didn't screw around, and charity directors didn't have their hands in the till. They were fine upstanding men – I was going to say men and women, but of course there weren't any women – who devoted their lives to serving the poor and vulnerable, and didn't screw them in any way at all. My parents' view doesn't have much traction these days.

Steve's the go-to guy in the bar when we want to know what young people think, which we don't much. He's twenty years or so younger than Marcie and me; younger than most of our customers. The fact that he's got two kids himself hasn't yet disqualified him from this role. Steve says we were naive to believe in the purity of our leaders, and why did we ever think they were better than the rest of us. Marcie and I point out that we never believed that: it was our parents, and their parents, who did. But Steve's basic point is right: things have changed.

We disagree on how things have changed, though. Steve says that people used to know nothing of the lives of the rich and powerful, but assumed the best. He thinks that these days we see more clearly how they are. Marcie and I think we still know nothing, and now assume the worst. We're the proponents of perpetual human ignorance. Steve's the proponent of greater insight through less deference and more information. That's another point of disagreement. Steve thinks that more information means more truth. We think it means guesses and lies being disseminated more widely.

All this business concerning Nelson's past or otherwise got to be relevant that August night, when he and Mike and I were alone in the bar. I need to explain the layout of the place first. When you walk up the few steps from the parking lot to the building, you enter a sort of vestibule. On the left is a corridor leading to the restrooms. On the right is a room with the ironic sign 'Office' on the door: not much more than a cupboard, with a desk and a chair, and stacked with boxes of merchandise. Ahead of you are the swing doors that lead into the bar room, the counter facing you. All I do in the office is add up the takings and prepare the banking. I keep the room locked, of course.

Usually, I count the previous day's takings early in the morning, or else during the lunch hour when Marcie's in charge. With Marcie away, and Alvin's funeral, and one thing and another, I hadn't done the cash for a few days. That evening presented the perfect opportunity to catch up, with a near empty bar room and Nelson in full monologue. I removed myself from proceedings and went to the office. I should think there was getting on for three grand sitting in the drawer.

After twenty minutes or so, Nelson poked his head round the door and asked if I could pour him and Mike another drink. Sure thing, I said. The barrel was empty, so I had to go change it in the cellar. For some reason, when I left the office, I didn't lock the door. Laziness, if I'm honest, but there were just the two customers and I would have my eyes on both of them, not that I thought I needed to. By the time I found I had to change the barrel, I'd forgotten about the office. I suppose I was gone five minutes. As I came back up to the bar, Nelson was coming through the swing doors. I assumed he'd been to the restroom.

I poured him and Mike a beer, then went back to counting the take. The take had gone. On the desk was a pile of loose change and no bills. In more than twenty years, I'd never lost a cent, and now this. I sat at the desk for a while, feeling sick to the stomach, trying to work out what to do. I wished Marcie was there. Two heads are better than one, and her head is better than mine in situations like this. I do one of two things. Either nothing – mull the problem over for a while, by which time the opportunity for instant action has passed – or something I regret later.

Whichever way I looked at matters, they pointed in a single direction. Nelson had stolen the money. In theory, there were two suspects. I had known Mike since we were kids and would trust him with my life. Nelson had the reputation of being a thief, had come into the office and seen the cash on the desk, and had been walking through the swing doors when I came up from the cellar. He could as well have been coming from the office as from the restroom. There could be only one conclusion.

In other circumstances, I might have called the cops. I couldn't see the point. The culprit was sitting in the bar room and the money couldn't be far away. The question was how to separate Mike from Nelson. Mike solved the problem by getting up to go. When he'd left, Nelson made moves to follow him.

'Hold on,' I said. 'We've got things to talk about.'

'Have we?' said Nelson. 'What things?'

'The money you stole.'

'What money?'

'The notes I was counting in the office. The notes you saw when you came to ask for a drink. The notes you took when I was changing the barrel.'

Nelson stared at me. 'Yes,' he said. 'I saw the notes. There was a big pile of them. Where do you suppose they are now?' He stood up and spread his arms. 'Do you want to frisk me? Would you like to say where you think I might be concealing them? You'd need a large bag for those bills.'

'I didn't say you had them on you. They could be in your car, for all I know.'

'OK. Let's go outside and look in my car.'

'I didn't say they were definitely in your car. They could be hidden in the bushes. I don't know where you put them. What I'm saying is that you took them.'

'So. While you changed the barrel, I went out and fetched a holdall from somewhere, came back to your office and stuffed it with notes, went outside to hide it someplace, then came back to the bar room as you returned. Is that what you're saying?'

'That's right.'

'You're crazy,' said Nelson.

'What's your explanation?'

'I don't need an explanation. It's your problem. Why don't you ask Mike?'

'Did he leave the room?'

'Easy for me to say yes,' said Nelson. 'I'm tempted to. But no, he didn't.'

'So what am I supposed to think?'

'You can think what you like. What I want to know is why you jumped to the conclusion it was me. You didn't know whether Mike had left the room until I just told you. You haven't asked whether anyone else came in and went out while you were downstairs. You assumed I stole your money. And, before you say anything, I know why you assumed it.

'I know the stories Stephanie tells. I know she and Marcie see each other. I've always presumed that you and Marcie were aware of the rumours. I've also presumed that you don't believe them. Plainly I was wrong. Things that never happened become as much facts as things that did happen. And there's nothing I can do. Someone invents stories for malicious reasons, and that's it. Nobody asks for my opinion. Nobody considers my point of view. Things fester in the background until an event like this happens, and then I get the blame. I hoped I'd avoided that here. It seems I haven't.'

'This has got nothing to do with Marcie,' I said.

'I know that. Marcie's too smart to make the sort of accusation you've made without a shred of evidence. Your trouble is, when Marcie's absent, so is your brain.'

This was not going the way I'd expected. Nelson sounded so outraged, I was close to believing him. However, I didn't believe him. There was no other explanation for what had happened. Crooks and liars like Nelson get away with it because they turn on the tap of righteous indignation so convincingly. I'd fallen for that sort of con in the past, and I wasn't going to fall for it again. It didn't alter the fact that I had no idea what to say or do next. It turned out that Nelson hadn't finished.

'I'll tell you three things,' he said. 'The first is that I am never coming back to this bar. The second is that, if I find you've been repeating your accusation to anyone, my lawyers will trash you. The third thing is that, before I go, you have the liberty to search me and my property for the cash. I will turn out my pockets. I will strip naked so you can see how many bills are stuffed up my backside. I will dismantle the car for you. Say what you want me to do.'

None of those things, for a start. I didn't think they'd be on offer if I was going to find anything. Unless it was bluff and bravado on Nelson's part. For some reason, I didn't feel inclined to call his bluff.

'I'll get a flashlight,' I said. 'Let's see what we find in the bushes round the parking lot.'

'Listen, you moron,' said Nelson. 'Someone took your money. I'm not accusing you of inventing the story. If there's a bag in the bushes, it proves nothing. Anyone could have put it there.'

I couldn't argue with that. We glared at each other for half a minute or more.

'If that's it,' said Nelson, 'I'll be going. It was good while it lasted.'

When he'd gone, I fetched the flashlight and searched the bushes on my own. I combed them four or five times and found nothing. I also checked my office from top to bottom. The money wasn't there. I had the brainwave that Nelson had put the notes in a plastic bag and left them in one of the cisterns in the restrooms. He hadn't. The evening ended at two in the morning with me short of three grand, one of my best customers, and any clue as to what had happened.

I barely slept that night, and felt awful the next morning. Marcie was due back late in the evening. I wanted her back that instant, even if I was going to get chewed off. Someone needed to make sense of it for me. I needed to talk about it. I also needed to be careful: I took Nelson's threat of lawyers seriously. Mike came in after work. Since he was the only other witness, and the one regular I could trust to keep his mouth shut, I decided to talk to him. I gave him a full account of the previous evening, missing out Nelson's possible back-story. I didn't know if Mike was aware of the rumours.

'Shit,' said Mike.

'Exactly.'

'I'm glad you didn't think it might be me.'

'I'd never think that for a minute, Mike.'

'Or else I'd have to find another bar too.' He smiled.

'Sorry, Mike,' I said. 'My sense of humour's gone AWOL for the moment.'

He pondered the story for a while. 'I can't make sense of it,' he said. 'I'm not surprised you came to that conclusion. Although . . . '

'Although what?'

'If one of us had done it, it was a hell of a chance to take. Nelson's not poor. Why risk his job and a criminal record for a few grand? How could he know how long you'd be?'

'Except,' I said, 'that – if it was him – he's got away with it, hasn't he? Takes it. Puts it somewhere on neutral territory, goodness knows where, then challenges me to prove it was him.'

'That's a lot to improvise in a few minutes.'

'How long was he out of the room?'

'I don't know,' said Mike. 'I wasn't paying attention. I'd say a minute or two. It could have been three or four, I suppose.'

'Who else could it have been?'

'Search me,' said Mike. 'No, don't. I haven't got anything up my backside, I assure you. The answer I want to give is Franky because, when anything happens that shouldn't, he's the first person who springs to mind.'

Mike knew Franky as well as I did. The three of us had been in the same class at school, the same group that did things together, then and afterwards. Mike had been cordial to Franky since he'd come back, but he'd put a distance into their relationship.

'Franky wasn't here.'

'No. Exactly. So I'm baffled. Do you remember those old locked-room puzzles? You know – a locked room with no windows, and when the door's forced, there's a dead body, some broken glass, a pool of water, and no one in the room. Explain it.'

'I can't,' I said. 'I don't remember that one.'

'The body was a goldfish,' said Mike. 'There was no person in the room, but there was a cat. The cat knocked over the goldfish bowl.'

'Why didn't the cat eat the goldfish?'

'I guess the cat was vegetarian.'

'This isn't getting us anywhere,' I said.

'It might be. What I'm saying is that there could be a different explanation that hasn't occurred to us.'

'Well, I wish it would,' I said. 'And quickly.'

'Did you ever hear rumours about Nelson and missing money?' asked Mike.

'Yes. I didn't know if you had, so I didn't mention it.'

'I didn't believe them at the time,' said Mike. 'But it makes you think, doesn't it?'

'Did you like Nelson?'

'Not that much,' said Mike. 'I can't say I'll miss him.'

'Nor will I.'

Marcie got back shortly after eight that evening. She'd been driving all day and was exhausted and hungry, and drained as she always was after that trip. I felt guilty again for not accompanying her, for never accompanying her, as well as for what had happened in her absence. I left the bar to Steve, who looked disappointed, because he wanted to hear how Marcie was after her trip, as he always did. I took her to our rooms and fed her and sat her down and asked her how it had been. I told her about Great-uncle Alvin's death and funeral, and made up my mind to leave the rest of my news to the next day. It never works that way with Marcie, though.

'What's the matter, honey?'

'Nothing,' I said.

'What's on your mind?'

'Nothing that can't wait till tomorrow.'

'I think you should tell me now, don't you?'

So I did. In full, and much of the time in tears. It had become too much for me, yet she should have been the one in need of consolation.

'I screwed up,' I said. 'I've lost us money and I've lost us Nelson. Apart from failing to lock the door, I don't know how I screwed up. I wish you'd been here.'

'Let's go to bed,' said Marcie, 'and see how things look in the morning.'

Marcie's always one for seeing how things look in the morning. She seems to have a filing clerk in her brain that sorts everything out in a neat, logical way while she's asleep. I have a troop of monkeys in my brain that scatters everything to the winds. I prefer to go on talking about things at night. But, on this occasion, my thoughts were addled enough without the aid of the monkeys, so I agreed to let the filing clerk take charge.

Not surprisingly, things didn't look much different to me in the morning. Worse, if anything. Marcie returned to the issue over breakfast, made me retell the story, asked me some questions.

'You don't think it was Nelson, do you?' I asked.

'No,' said Marcie. 'I don't.'

'Why not?'

'I agree with what Mike said. To conceive that on the spur of the moment is beyond belief. Beyond Nelson, anyway. And he would have known he'd be the main suspect, maybe the only suspect. Why do it?'

'I know that,' I said. 'Give me another explanation.'

166

'Why should we assume that the thief ever came into the bar room?'

'What do you mean?'

'Why couldn't the thief have come from outside, gone into the office, taken the cash and left again?'

'You're saying that some stranger, who happens to be passing, stops at the bar on the off chance there's a pile of cash sitting there unattended, and takes it.'

'I didn't say anything about a stranger,' said Marcie. She looked at me.

'Oh, I see,' I said. 'I get it. Why does everything have to be Franky's fault?'

'Because it usually is.'

'Tell me what you think happened.'

'I don't know what happened,' said Marcie. 'I'm trying to figure out what might have happened. How late was this?'

'Quite late.'

'Was it dark?'

'Yes.'

'So the light would have been on in your office.'

'Yes,' I said.

'Was Franky's car in the parking lot?'

'It was there when I was looking in the shrubs around midnight. I've no idea whether it was there earlier. I don't think I went outside all day. Besides, I wouldn't have seen it unless I went behind our house, and I only did that when I was searching the bushes.'

'Suppose,' said Marcie, 'Franky's been out and comes back just as you've gone down to change the barrel. You wouldn't have heard him. He sees a light in your office and comes in, to have a drink, or to say hello. He puts his head round the office door, sees the cash and takes it. Pure opportunism. It would have taken a couple of minutes or less. Then it's back to Mr Hammond's house, hide the cash and sit there looking cool, in case you come calling. Tell me why that couldn't have happened.'

'It would have taken some nerve on Franky's part,' I said.

'It took some nerve on the part of whoever did it. I'd back Franky over Nelson when it comes to nerve. Wouldn't you?'

'The fact is,' I said, 'that you don't like Franky, so he gets the blame for everything. Why don't we give him a break for once?'

'The fact is,' said Marcie, 'that you don't like Nelson much. And we shouldn't forget the question of motive. I can't think why Nelson would be mad enough to do such a thing. Whereas it was only a couple of weeks ago that we were asking ourselves how Franky was financing his building works, and wondering who'd been gullible enough to wind up as his banker. Turns out it was us.'

11

Arlene and Davy the second time around was not the same as Arlene and Davy the first time. They'd split up for no more than a fortnight, in the first half of July, but the furniture got rearranged during the interlude. I've done the bit about kissing and allowing to be kissed. There was also the issue about leaving and being left, and who was going to do which, and why.

In retrospect, they hadn't made a 'let's get back together' decision, they'd made a 'let's figure out a better time to end it' decision. By late September, they'd been together the second time for nearly as long as they had been the first time, but it had become casual. There was no intensity to it. Both of them were marking time, waiting for something that wasn't yet ready to happen. That was how it appeared.

By this time, we had two portraits of Davy. The first, a self-portrait by the artist, was little more than a doodle. This depicted a single man, never married, who had come to town for reasons that remained unclear, and who had since performed a variety of jobs, none of them commensurate with his age or intelligence. This sketch had never convinced.

You'd have to call the second one a self-portrait too. Although it was painted by Arlene, the image was dictated by Davy. We had gleaned it from Arlene at odd moments over the course of several months. This was Davy as he would like to be seen by Arlene, so was no more reliable than the first portrait. It did, however, contain more detail than the first. You could call it impressionistic. An ex-wife had been added to the composition, although no detail on her, or any children. A previous life in Ohio had been supplied. A narrative that involved a messy divorce settlement and assorted other components of a hard-luck story had been woven into the fabric. Exactly what you'd expect, if you were aiming for the sympathy vote.

This portrait was even less convincing. The first was merely unsatisfactory, but it could have been true. At the time, we didn't know for certain that it wasn't. The second portrait told us that the first one was a lie, at least with respect to Davy's marital history, which was a big respect. So the second one could have been a lie too, as could any subsequent portrait. Soon as you tell one lie, you might as well be telling thousands. Everybody knows this except politicians. Politicians and Davy Brewster.

I had gone fishing for a few days in mid-September, like I do every year. Not far away, but far enough to stay away from home. Most years, it was a healing time. Not this year. I couldn't help but dwell on how the deaths of Roseanne and Bobby had made life come so close to unravelling, of the effort it had taken, from Marcie and from me, to stop it doing so. We had gathered the yards of string that lay strewn around us. We had patiently teased out the knots, and wound the string tightly around its spindle. Wound it so tightly that nothing could unravel it again.

Since Franky's return, the ball of string had begun to be picked loose. Whatever world Marcie and I inhabited, it had been our world, and we shared it. Now, plots had become fenced off. There were areas we could no longer inhabit together. This part was my area. That part was Marcie's. What had once been common land was being parcelled up and sold off to developers. We hadn't done it. This was Franky's work, deft and designed to look unplanned. I feared where this might lead, as long as he was around. It was not a happy trip for me. And I didn't catch many fish.

Soon after I was back, another artist came through the bar room doors and offered a further portrait of Davy.

She was good-looking, in a conventional way. As if God had taken the average of every Caucasian nose in the country and given it to her, then done the same with eyes and mouth and hair and the rest of the female body. God hadn't left it at the physical attributes; he'd sketched in a personality. He'd given her a look of average intelligence, which turned out to be an understatement. And he'd given her a toothpaste smile, but taken care to balance it with a hint of pain behind the eyes. Quite a lot of pain, in fact. God had overdone that part. Or maybe not. I don't know how her life had been.

She stood in the centre of the bar and looked around her, rotating slowly like the lantern of a lighthouse, favouring each angle of vision in turn with her beam. She gave out the attitude of someone who didn't spend much time in bars but wasn't about to be overawed by the fact. The attitude of someone whose very stare would compel the attendance of whoever she was seeking. In that respect, she failed. The person wasn't there and refused to materialize for the moment. She approached me as a consolation prize.

'Hi,' she said. 'I'm looking for Davy Brewster.' Her long, mid-brown hair fell across her face. Pantone reference 18-1033, I should say.

'And you are?' I never admitted to a stranger that I knew a customer.

'Mary-Jane Brewster.'

Well, I'll be darned. Here was the face in the other photo frame in Davy's apartment: the one that had not been smashed up. Davy's ex had shown up in town, still using his name these two years later. Or that could have been for my benefit, to establish her place in the constellations.

'He's not here,' I said.

'I can see that. Are you expecting him? I'm told he's in here most nights.'

'I don't know if he'll be in.' At this point, I didn't like her attitude. Surely it's not possible to be aggressive and obsequious at the same time. Mary-Jane managed it. Later, when I decided her attitude was the best thing about her, I put it down to nerves.

'You do know him?'

'Sure,' I said. 'But I don't know whether he's likely to be in tonight, or tomorrow night or any particular night.'

'Do you know where he lives?'

'No idea.' I expect she knew I was lying.

'I'll wait awhile,' she said. 'Could I have a Coke, please?'

'Sure thing.'

I thought she'd take her drink to a vacant table and sit there looking spare. She didn't. She clambered on to a stool at the bar, Arlene's stool as it happened, and attempted to engage me in conversation. I was happy to oblige.

'It's a nice bar you've got here,' said Mary-Jane.

'Thank you,' I said. 'You live in town?'

'No.' She seemed surprised to be asked, which was what I intended. 'I live in Ohio. I'm visiting.'

'Oh. You Davy's sister or something?'

'No. I'm his wife.'

Not 'ex-wife', note: 'wife'.

'Didn't know he was married,' I said. Quite justified,

that remark, in my opinion. Davy had told me he wasn't married. He should know.

'You don't seem to know much,' said Mary-Jane. She smiled.

'Almost nothing,' I said. 'You're right. He's here a lot. We talk about all sorts of things; not too much about our own lives.'

'Does he come on his own?'

'Sure. He comes on his own.'

That was a factual answer, and I was entitled to give it, wasn't I? Davy did come on his own. He came on his own and he left with Arlene. Mary-Jane hadn't asked who he left with. All right. I wasn't entitled to say it. I wasn't entitled to answer the question. Mary-Jane knew that, which was why she asked it. As a test. This was the moment when our conversation became complicit. She wanted information from me and I wanted it from her. We had now signalled our mutual intention to do business. It wasn't a question of pumping each other. Neither of us needed to do that. We left the faucets ajar and stuff leaked out.

'Has he been in any fights?' asked Mary-Jane.

'He arrived in a fight,' I said. 'That was a couple of years ago. He hasn't been in one since. Not in here, anyhow.'

'Is he working?'

'Yes,' I said. 'But . . .'

'. . . but what?'

'It's none of my business. Davy is a smart guy and he's had an education, so I'm surprised at the sort of work he does. I should have thought he could get something better.'

'What's he doing?'

'He's foreman in a warehouse right now. It changes quite often.'

Mary-Jane bit her lip and looked thoughtful. 'Once upon a time, he was a sales director,' she said. 'And now he's got a job in a warehouse. Does he work in town?'

'Hereabouts,' I said. 'Look, Mrs Brewster, I'd like to help you as much as I can. But I don't know that Davy wants to see you, so I'm not going to tell you where he works, or where he lives.'

'I understand that,' she said, and bit her lip again. 'Would you say he was happy?'

I should have known the answer to that question. I didn't. The answer I wanted to give was, 'He ought to be,' but then I'd have had to explain why, and I wasn't going to do that. Both Davy and Arlene should have been happy. I didn't feel that either of them was. With Arlene, I think it was temperamental. Everything suggested someone who didn't have the talent for being happy. With Davy, I didn't know what it was.

'I think he's OK,' I said. 'Medium happy, I'd say.'

It was hard to tell whether that answer pleased Mary-Jane. I got the impression that she wanted Davy to be happy in principle, but would rather he wasn't happy at this moment. She minded: that was undeniable.

'I think I'll head off,' she said. 'I expect I'll be back quite soon.'

'If Davy comes in, do you want me to tell him you were here?'

Mary-Jane smiled. 'I should think you'll tell him anyway, won't you?'

'If I do see him, is there a message you'd like me to pass on?'

'Yes,' she said, 'there is. You can tell him it's time he mailed me some more money. The deal was I got some every month. There hasn't been a cent for weeks. I don't know who or what he's spending it on. It's time some of it came to his family. You can also tell him to stop beating himself up. You can tell him to come home and get on with the life we used to have. If you want, you can tell him . . . No, I'd better say that myself. Finally, you can tell him that I'm hanging around here until I can say all this and more to his face. The grandparents are looking after the kids for the time being. That's Davy's parents, by the way. I'm in no hurry. I've got at least a week here and it won't take me that long to find him. I'm asking you to be the messenger so he can get used to the idea that I'm in town, and won't lose his temper when he sees me.'

'Does he usually?'

'He's been known to.'

'Why did he leave?'

'He can tell you himself, if he wants to. Obviously he doesn't, or he'd have told you already. Let's say it was pride. Tons of it. Who's that?'

'Who's who?'

Mary-Jane jerked her head. 'That woman who's walked in. The one over there. The tarty one.'

'Oh,' I said. 'That's Arlene.'

'Is it just?' she said.

She knew. I swear she knew. Don't ask me how, but she did. Come to think of it, how did she know Davy drank in here? Someone had been talking to her. Whoever it was must have told her about Arlene.

Mary-Jane vacated Arlene's stool, walked toward the door, eyeing its usual occupant on the way. Arlene took her accustomed seat the moment that Mary-Jane had gone.

'I see you've got yourself a new girlfriend.'

'I should be so lucky.'

'Who is she?'

'Mary-Jane.'

The name registered with Arlene straightaway. 'Not Davy's wife?' she said.

'That's the one.' I filled her in on our conversation.

'Oh, wow,' said Arlene. 'That's incredible. I wish I'd come in earlier. You could have introduced us.'

I stared at her. I expect my jaw dropped. I know

Arlene was a little crazy at the best of times, but come on. I decided she was being ironic.

'Yeah, the two of you could have gone ten rounds right here in the bar.'

'I don't think you get it,' said Arlene. 'I don't mind.'

'You must.'

'I don't. It's not as if I'm in love with Davy. You know that, don't you? I like him; I like spending time with him. It's been good to have someone in my life. And that's all it is. He feels the same. There's nothing long term about us. Besides, Davy is in love with Mary-Jane. He talks of her constantly. I've told him he ought to go back to her.'

'What does he say?'

'He says she wouldn't have him.'

'Why? What's he done?'

'He doesn't say. It could be big and he's ashamed of it. Or it could be small and he wants me to think it's big.'

'Mary-Jane wants him back,' I said. 'She said so herself. And she wants Davy to stop beating himself up about whatever it is he beats himself up about.'

'Which is what I don't know,' said Arlene.

'Mary-Jane knows who you are.'

'She can't.'

'She does.' I told Arlene the conversation.

'There's only one person could have told her.'

Arlene expected me to know who that was. I didn't. 'Who?' I had to ask.

'Davy.'

'Why would he tell Mary-Jane about you?'

'Search me,' said Arlene.

'It must have been to make her jealous,' I said. 'Seems to have worked. She's come here at the first opportunity.'

'Yeah. Maybe,' said Arlene. 'That figures.'

'Why do you seem so detached, Arlene?'

'Because I am detached. I'm fond of Davy. I don't love him. I told you. There's no reason not to want him to be happy. I reckon he'd be happier with Mary-Jane. I want him to go back to her.'

'Very noble,' I said.

'It isn't noble. It's common sense. Life's hard enough as it is.'

'Are you expecting Davy tonight?' I asked.

'Sure.' We heard the sound of a car door shutting. 'I expect that'll be him now.'

It wasn't. It was Mary-Jane again. Her car wouldn't start, she said later. Like hell, it wouldn't. She'd been sitting in the seat debating how brave she wanted to be. She decided to be eleven brave on a scale of ten. She walked straight toward the counter, toward the two of us, and introduced herself to Arlene.

'Hi,' she said. 'I'm Mary-Jane Brewster. Davy is my husband.'

'Why don't we go and sit at a table?' said Arlene. 'Can I get you a drink?'

I wasn't best pleased with Arlene for cutting me out

of the loop like that. This was going to be a major conversation. I could tell because Arlene ordered a vodka Martini and Mary-Jane a bourbon. A few minutes after I'd put their drinks on the table and got back to the bar, the doors opened again and in walked Davy. He stood there, mouth open, watching his wife talking to his lover. The two women didn't see him. They were yattering to each other, oblivious to all else. I shrugged my shoulders at Davy as if to say that this had nothing to do with me.

Davy stood there, unsteadily. He'd already started drinking, from the look of it. He was some yards away from the women, not in their direct line of vision. In any case, they were too engrossed to look up. They were looking into eyes, behind eyes, around eyes, through eyes, translating body language, evaluating clothes and make-up, assessing age and work done to disguise it. Decoding each other, the way you do when you meet a stranger who turns out to be part of your story. Davy must have stood there for two or three minutes. Then he turned on his heels and walked out through the doors. I gave him a while to make his getaway, before sidling up to the women to get revenge for my exclusion.

'Davy was in here a moment ago,' I said. That remark didn't sink in for several seconds.

'What did you say?' asked Mary-Jane, when it did.

'I said Davy was in here a moment ago.'

'Where?'

'Right here.'

'Why didn't you say so?'

'Didn't like to interrupt,' I said. 'And I assumed you'd recognize him.'

There was plenty to chew over with Marcie later that night. From memory, the gnawing went on till one in the morning. Why did Mary-Jane come to find Davy? Who told her where to find him? Why did Mary-Jane and Arlene look more like friends than rivals for Davy's affections? We ranged over these topics without being any the wiser by the end of it. I stuck to my opinion that Davy was the one who had told Mary-Jane where to find him.

'Why didn't he go over and talk to her, in that case?' asked Marcie. 'And why did he look so astonished when he saw her?'

'He wasn't astonished at that. He was astonished at finding her talking to Arlene.'

'If someone wants to reopen negotiations with an ex-wife they haven't seen in two years, who would choose to do it in a public bar?' said Marcie. 'And who would do it without arranging a date and a time? It makes no sense. It wasn't Davy.'

'If it wasn't Davy,' I said, 'it must have been at Mary-Jane's instigation. She must have got some private dick to track him down. If someone's been spying on Davy around here, that would account for her knowing about Arlene.'

'Quite possible. Assuming it wasn't the usual suspect.'

'How could it have been?'

'Oh,' said Marcie, 'that's just me. If a mystery arises when Franky's around, he's a suspect as far as I'm concerned. And the more difficult it is to see his motive, the more suspicious I become. He'd be quite happy to have Davy out of the way. He wants Arlene for himself.'

'When I was at the school,' I said, 'us teachers would spend hours trying to discover who was responsible for the latest prank. We could never find out. Eventually, we decided it was a waste of our time. So we appointed an official school scapegoat and, whenever anything went wrong, it was the fault of the scapegoat. That was a brilliant system, and I see you've decided to adopt it here, dearest. Whatever can't be explained is down to Franky. Let's blame him for everything.'

'It would certainly save a lot of time,' said Marcie.

We never got to the bottom of how Mary-Jane came to the bar, or what she discussed with Arlene. The fact is we knew nothing about nothing. We didn't have half the pieces of the puzzle. We didn't have a quarter.

If I'm not mistaken, there are places in the world where people submit to arranged marriages. Sounds a weird concept to me, but I'm told it's true. What was happening here was an arranged separation, and it accelerated after Mary-Jane's appearance. Arlene and Davy were making the arrangements directly with each other, in a most considerate manner, and with no suggestion that their emotions were engaged, which they must have been, mustn't they?

The truth about Davy, or the closest we were likely to get to it, began to emerge in the process. Mary-Jane was the physical proof he'd been married, as Arlene had already told us. We now knew that the picture in his wallet was of his kids, not of his niece and nephew. We didn't know why the marriage had ended, specially seeing as how Davy and Mary-Jane gave a good impression of still being in love with each other.

Guess who flung most of the missing pieces of the puzzle down on the table? Arlene. That's right. The woman who would tell us next to nothing about herself came up with the goods on Davy. It happened during the twilight weeks when we were expecting Davy and Arlene to split for the second time. During those weeks, they were in the bar most nights, not always together or at the same time. It had become a syncopated affair, and neither seemed bothered by that fact.

One evening, Arlene sat on her stool at the counter, one high-heeled leg slung over the other, and Marcie sat on another stool, one slippered leg slung over the other, and the three of us were jawing. Marcie chucked the name of Mary-Jane into the conversation, like you might a can of gasoline on to a bonfire. There was no explosion. What it did was to start Arlene off on Davy and his previous life. Yet another version of his previous life, and not one that bore much relationship to what Davy had told Arlene before. This is the gist of it.

Davy and Mary-Jane had married early. Both had

good jobs. Davy was sales manager for a large corporation, later its sales director. Mary-Jane did research at a healthcare company. They had a son and a daughter, like you do. Everything was hunky-dory as far as anyone could tell. As far as Davy himself could tell, as a matter of fact. His life was idyllic. Bluebirds glided over the mountain and roses bloomed round the cottage door, allowing for the fact that they lived on an executive estate in a small town outside Cincinnati.

One day everything fell apart. Davy told Arlene he had felt like a pressure cooker, water boiling to a scream within his system for months, the whistle on top blowing like a steam engine, till one day the whole darn thing erupted. The guy who caught the blast was his neighbour. Arlene couldn't remember what the neighbour had done to annoy Davy. Some insubstantial misdemeanour, she thought, like blocking his driveway, or raking leaves on to his lawn. Not the sort of offence for which you expect to get beaten to a pulp, which was what happened.

That was at ten o'clock on a Saturday morning. The police assumed he'd been drinking, or was drunk from the night before. But Davy was sober. He just blew. The cops didn't buy that. People losing it for no apparent reason was not within their comprehension, although cops do it themselves on a regular basis. Cops think they're special, having to deal with stuff that no one else has to deal with, so they mitigate their own shortcomings, but not other people's.

Davy wasn't inside for long: a few months, Arlene thought. It wasn't the time that mattered, it was the collateral damage. The effect on Davy's family, on his livelihood, on the poor bastard of a neighbour, on Davy himself. What he couldn't get his head around was that this was an arbitrary event. An event that happened, but might equally not have happened. With that one punch, or several punches to be clear about it, his life fell apart.

There was the jail term for an appetizer: his employers weren't impressed by that. The job went immediately and his résumé now featured a criminal record, so getting a new one wasn't easy, which was why the jobs weren't as good as they should have been. When he was released, Mary-Jane asked him to move out of the house for a while. Davy had no idea what had made him flip in the first place, according to Arlene. He knew he could have done with some therapy. There was no money for that by then, and no employer to pay for it.

The neighbourhood went too. It was where Davy lived, and also where he had grown up. It was home to him. Even if he could have afforded another place there, which he couldn't, no one would have wanted to be his neighbour. He was persona non grata in that town. That was when he moved here. Arlene didn't know why he chose this town. It's not as if it's that close to Cincinnati. Maybe that was why. He couldn't get a proper job. Most of his earnings went to pay for the kids, and for the upkeep of a home he never visited. He hadn't seen his children since it happened.

In the space of a few minutes on an ordinary Saturday morning, Davy's life had changed, completely and for ever. More than the inventory of the individual things he'd lost, it was the entirety of what he'd lost, and the speed of its exodus, that weighed heaviest on him, Arlene said. All he could ask, which he did, over and over, was why did he go to talk to the neighbour that morning? Why didn't he go to the grocery store with Mary-Jane, like he usually did? Arlene said he would sit there and go, 'Why? why? why? why?' a hundred times over.

Arlene said she'd been a therapist for Davy, in an informal kind of way. What she couldn't fathom was his anger. If it had been caused by what had happened to him, that would be understandable, even if it was his own fault. Davy told her that the anger was already there, which figures, since he wouldn't have belted his neighbour otherwise. And he swore it was there before his kids, and before his marriage, and before his job. He swore it had been there for as long as he could remember. Marcie said something must have happened to him as a kid. Arlene said Davy swore it hadn't; his childhood had been fine. He may not have been telling the truth, of course. People don't about things like that.

'When did Mary-Jane divorce him?' Marcie asked Arlene.

'She didn't. They're still legally married. I found that

out recently. Kind of puts a different perspective on things, don't you think?'

'Did she try to stop him seeing the kids?'

'I don't think so,' said Arlene. 'Not that Davy said.'

'Then why did he move all the way over here?' I asked.

'I know only what I told you.'

'Do you believe his story?'

'I believe most of it,' said Arlene. 'Not every last bit of it. I think he's frightened he'll do it again, and that next time it will be Mary-Jane or the kids. Perhaps she did ask him to move out for a while, but not for good, and not so far away. I think Davy chose to do that to punish himself. I think what's been going on in the past week or so has been Mary-Jane telling him to stop beating himself up and to go back home.'

'And?' asked Marcie.

'And he will, as long as the Supreme Court that's in session in his head right now tells him he can. It's what he wants to do.'

'What about you?'

'I'm OK. Life goes on. It was never going anywhere, was it?' I wasn't sure whether Arlene was referring to life or to her relationship with Davy.

'Has he helped you look for Jack?'

'No,' said Arlene. 'Davy isn't interested in Jack.' She looked at her watch. 'I don't think he's coming tonight, do you?'

187

A night or two later, we told Mike what we'd heard. Arlene hadn't said we shouldn't, and since Mike had heard the lies, it was fair he should now hear the truth. Assuming it was the truth. Mike fancies himself as a philosopher. He said that everybody's life changes for ever, for one reason or another. It's only when it's a positive action, like it was with Davy, that anyone remarks upon it. Usually it's a passive action that does it, the failure to do something that might change things for the better, or at least change them. Those things go unnoticed. Marcie and I looked at each other when he said that.

There's a time to give out information, the good book says, and a time to refrain from giving out information. It doesn't say that, but it would be in keeping with the general tenor of the argument. After two years of not knowing much about Davy, and not trusting what we did know, we now felt informed. After many months of knowing next to nothing about Arlene, we were about to learn one or two things that might have meant something. It was hard to be sure. Arlene was a Mr Hammond-type figure. You could make up what you liked about Arlene, or she could make it up about herself, and no one could say for sure whether it was true. The messenger was Davy.

'She certainly spent time there,' he said. I'd asked him whether she really came from Pittsburgh. It seemed a good idea to start at the beginning. 'I know Pittsburgh a little myself. She says she lived there for a few years, and she knows enough of the city to make that possible. That story she told of the man in the apartment across the street whom she was fixed on. She said that was in Pittsburgh.'

'Was she born there?'

'There or thereabouts was what she said. Typical Arlene answer.'

'Doesn't her passport tell her?'

'She says she hasn't got one. She's never been out of the country.'

'She must have some document that says when and where she was born,' said Marcie. 'What about a birth certificate?'

'I didn't ask,' said Davy. 'It was clear she didn't want to talk about it. I guess people are entitled to their privacy.'

'Did you discover anything about her father?' I asked.

'Nope. She said she never knew him. He must have left home when she was very young, assuming he was ever at home.'

'You have to admit,' I said, 'that, if you were someone who liked to keep people guessing, you couldn't invent a better history.'

'True,' said Davy. 'And you also have to admit that, if you were a rootless and insecure person, you might have a history like this one.'

'You think she's like that?'

'Sure,' said Davy. 'Don't you?'

'Most of the time, yes. Then she says something, or does something, that suggests the opposite. So I don't know. I've given up trying to figure out Arlene's psychology. I'd settle for a few facts.'

'We don't have any,' said Davy. 'We don't know whether she's as ignorant as she claims, or whether she's not saying. None of us knows Jack shit.'

'Speaking of Jack, what did you discover about him?'

'Zilch. To begin with, I often asked about him, but then I stopped. It was a pointless topic of conversation. She wasn't saying.'

'I discovered something,' I said.

'You did? When?'

'On Coney Island. She told me Jack used to send money to her mom. He mailed her cheques. They stopped about three years ago.'

'Her mom died long before that,' said Davy.

'I know, but Jack apparently didn't. He went on sending the cheques, and Arlene went on cashing them. Jack's a mystery man from her past. That's why she wants to find him. Assuming he's still alive, which it sounds as though he isn't.'

'In which case,' said Marcie, 'she may be chasing an inheritance. It sounds as though Jack had money.'

'Why is she looking for him here?' asked Davy.

'She gave the impression that the cheques were postmarked here. And in a few other places too. I don't think this is the only place she's looking. She's been spending time in the bastard town next door, for starters.'

'And perhaps in Indiana,' said Davy. 'If she really went there.'

'To be honest,' said Marcie, 'I'm getting a little tired of these guessing games.'

'Davy, old man,' I said. 'You've been carrying on with Arlene for six months now. Is there not a single thing you can tell us that you know to be true and that we don't know already?'

Davy considered the question, trying to avoid having to say no.

'There's one thing, I suppose. It's not much.'

'What is it?'

'A shopping list fell out of her purse a few weeks ago. From the look of it, I'd say it had been there a while. She'd torn off part of an envelope and written the list on the back. The envelope had an address in this town.'

'Street?'

'Pine.'

'Number?'

'7.'

'Do you know who lives there?'

'Of course I do. I checked. A woman called Mrs Riessen.'

'And what is she to Arlene?'

'I've no idea,' said Davy. 'I ought to add that the address was in Arlene's own handwriting. Just because it was written on an envelope, I don't think you can assume it had been used as an envelope. Since this happened, I've driven up Pine a few times. I've never seen Arlene there, and I've never seen her car.'

'So it doesn't tell us anything.'

'It tells us something. We just don't know what.'

That should have been Arlene's epitaph. I expect it will get carved on her tombstone one day.

12

When Davy and Arlene finally split up, it was Arlene who did the leaving. There are the leavers and the left in these situations, and Arlene was a leaver. It is assumed that they are the stronger ones. In my opinion, most leavers take the initiative because they are petrified of being abandoned.

Davy and Arlene left the bar together one Saturday evening. 'We're going up to Deadman's Wood tomorrow,' one of them said.

'Enjoy yourselves, then,' I said.

Hardly an inspired piece of dialogue. I wouldn't be mentioning it but for what happened next. They went to the wood separately, in their own cars, and spent an hour or two there. Then they kissed goodbye and Davy got back to his car and found the note on his seat.

'I don't know how she managed to put it there,' he said in the bar the next evening. 'Anyhow, she's not coming back.'

'You don't know that,' I said. 'She hasn't found Jack yet.'

'I have this image of her in Deadman's Wood,' said Davy. 'She went running off to catch falling leaves. She said it would bring us luck. I hadn't heard that superstition before. It hasn't brought us much luck, has it? Maybe it's brought Arlene some luck. Or maybe she never caught any leaves.'

I can't say I was surprised. Women like Arlene always leave. That's what they do. Hang around for a while and then blow away. Her life seemed to come in segments, like an orange. A membrane separated the parts, and one segment had no connection with the next. The continuity lady went missing when Arlene was born.

After such an event, the world likes to pontificate about why it happened, and when it began to happen, and how the pontificators noticed it before anyone else, although they didn't get round to mentioning it at the time. The slice of the world that inhabited my bar room expressed their opinions, and the gist of them was this. Some held that Davy changed toward Arlene from the moment that Mary-Jane tracked him down. The more devious believed that Davy had engineered this scenario to make Mary-Jane jealous and win her back. Others held that Arlene changed toward Davy from the moment that Franky first pitched up, a long while earlier. They were united in thinking that Arlene fancied Franky.

The aftermath was the reverse of what had happened the first time. Then there was melodrama, Davy metaphorically clutching his head and crying, 'Woe is me.' It didn't have the ring of truth, perhaps because it turned out not to be true. This time, the split had an air of finality, and there was no melodrama. You got the impression that Davy wasn't much bothered, and Arlene had spared him from having to do the leaving himself. Anyway, whether through stoicism or indifference, Davy didn't sit at home and mope. He was in the bar every evening, cheerful as you like.

Not long after, Mary-Jane showed up again. It was clear that she had met up with Davy in the meantime, goodness knows where or when.

Davy loved Mary-Jane, and Mary-Jane loved Davy. You can mystify things how you want and be as clever as you like, but sometimes it comes down to a thing that simple. Mary-Jane thought she couldn't forgive Davy for busting up the family, then found she had to because she loved him. Davy thought he couldn't forgive himself, then found he had to because he loved Mary-Jane, and she wanted him back. You can go to college and become a professor, but, however smart you are, the smartest you can be is when you stop looking for complicated explanations for simple things.

There was a winding down of affairs after that. Mary-Jane showed up a couple of times more. We chatted, and I liked her as I had the first time. I dropped into one of our conversations that she must have hired a good guy to track Davy down.

'That's a long story,' she said.

'Want to tell it?'

'Not especially. The important thing is that it's worked out well for everyone.'

And that's as much as she would say. She left for home soon after.

Davy was due to follow her to Cincinnati shortly. He'd terminated the lease on his apartment. I imagine the fumigation didn't come cheap. He'd given in his notice at the warehouse. He hadn't found a new position back in Ohio, but wasn't concerned about that. It's all in how you look at things. At another time, the lack of an income would have spooked Davy, as it does most people. Now, he had Mary-Jane back and he had his kids back and he had his home back, and nothing else mattered.

Davy was soaring. Sometime back, on Coney Island, when I'd asked Arlene what she and Davy talked about, she'd said they imagined what birds they'd be, if they were birds. Strange, since Arlene had no interest in birds. She said that Davy imagined himself as a phoenix, ready to rise from the fire. Not what I would have thought at the time. There must a brown, fidgety bird somewhere that flies into unprovoked rages. That would have been Davy then. Now he was soaring. Davy would shortly be taking flight. All passengers should proceed to the departure lounge. Good luck to him.

Nelson had departed; now Davy was gone too. No bar room in or near Cincinnati would get his custom: the fact is that solid family life is the sworn enemy of bar takings. We hadn't seen Arlene since the split with Davy. The rota of the absent was lengthening by the week, and before long it seemed to have claimed another name. I heard the news in town and rushed back to tell Marcie, even though it was the middle of the lunch hour.

'Guess what?' I said. I left a pause for dramatic effect. 'It looks like Franky's leaving town.'

'What makes you think that?'

'They told me down the gas station when I was filling the tank. He was with a blonde he met at the bowling alley. They told me that too. The guy said she was barely legal.'

'I should think "barely" is the right word for it.'

'He's got himself a new car. He's got white-walled wheels and a white-walled blonde. She was all over Franky, apparently. The guy said she was doing unmentionable things to him as they drove off.'

'I expect he mentioned them to you,' said Marcie.

'In passing,' I said. 'Lucky old Franky.'

'I wouldn't say so. The wheels will come off before long.'

'Off the car, or the blonde?'

'Both,' said Marcie. 'You can't go on Franky's way for ever. There's a limit to the number of dumb blondes in the world.'

'I'm not sure about that,' I said. 'And he hasn't yet started on the brunettes.' I shot Marcie a glance.

Marcie considered the news for a while. 'I expect we

financed the new car,' she said eventually. 'And the blonde as well.'

'Not for long. Blondes aren't cheap.'

'Franky's will be.'

'I don't pretend to understand it,' I said. 'All that time he's spent doing up Mr Hammond's place. Why would he want to leave town now?'

'He wouldn't. And he hasn't. This is just a fling until Arlene comes back. Those two have unfinished business. The blonde might expect it to last. Franky won't. He'll be back before long.'

All this has a kind of elegiac tone, as if there was a grand clear-out of the clientele. In a way there was, but it was nothing new. It had happened before. The cast of regulars had been reduced to one by early October, and boy, did Mike rejoice in the role. It was one monologue after another from him, and he'd been the quiet one. New regulars would arrive soon. There'd been life before Nelson and Davy: Jack Nightingale for a start. Arlene and Franky had monopolized thoughts and conversations, but they'd been around no more than six or eight months. The planets had appeared fixed in their heaven. That was an illusion. No one had pressed the pause button. Everything had kept churning. There had been new configurations, new triangulations, all the while. And Marcie and I were not the same people either.

It was a case of goodbye, hello, and on we go. The way it always has been.

Turned out, though, that Marcie was right about Franky and Arlene. In mid-October, a couple of weeks after Davy had left, I caught the sound of 'Theme from Dixie' coming from a car horn in the parking lot. Must once have been a Southern car. I looked out of the window and saw a Mustang with white-walled tyres. Franky was back in town. A woman was with him. She was not blonde, and was way too old for jailbait. I walked back to the counter and mixed a vodka Martini.

Franky walked in the way he usually did, like everyone in the world was his best friend and, if they weren't, he'd make them best friends by force of personality. Like he owned the place. Arlene walked in the way she usually didn't, like she was now the co-owner. She came close to a swagger. It crossed my mind that Franky had given her some drug, of the sort that alters your personality. She waltzed around the bar room, high-fiving everyone she knew, while Franky stood with thumbs in belt loops like the Fonz. Come on, Arlene, you've only been gone five minutes.

'You've got to hand it to Franky,' I said to Marcie later that night. 'He knows how to make a woman feel good about herself.'

'Nobody does it better. For the first five minutes.'

'It's funny,' I said, 'that Franky's parents didn't have more than one kid. How many Catholic families do you know with one kid?'

'Franky's parents didn't have any kids,' said Marcie. 'Franky was adopted.'

'What? I never knew that. You never told me that. That's why Franky's afraid of you. He thinks you know his secret, and you do.'

'No, no,' said Marcie. 'That's not a secret. Everybody knows it.'

'I don't.'

'Everybody except you. Believe me, it's not a secret. I'd have mentioned it ages ago, if I'd thought you didn't know.'

'How come he was adopted?'

'I don't know. Perhaps Mr and Mrs Albertino couldn't have kids.'

'Who were Franky's real parents? Does Franky know who they were?'

'No idea on either count,' said Marcie.

I don't like it when things get confused, because then I get confused, like I was now. Marcie embraces confusion. She thinks life is an endless battle between order and chaos. I agree with her there, but I'm not neutral in the fight, like she is. I'd beat chaos to a pulp if I could. I'm rooting for order. In this situation, there wasn't any.

I'd been debating things with myself since Franky had moved in next door and taken up his new role as Mr Hammond junior. Marcie couldn't see anything peculiar in it. To her, it was another of Franky's scams, another part of the chaos theory. To me, there had to be more behind it. I felt that Mr Hammond senior fitted into the picture somehow, and that he fitted into the same frame as Franky. Until now, I hadn't been able to see the connection. When Marcie mentioned that Franky was adopted, everything seemed to fall into place.

'Maybe Franky found his father,' I said.

'Who are you suggesting for the part?'

'Mr Hammond.'

'Why?'

'No specific reason,' I said. 'But something made Franky come back to town, and what was it otherwise? He hasn't come to see anyone in particular, as far as we can tell. He's not working, so far as we know. The one definite thing he's done since he came back is to occupy Mr Hammond's house. And change his name to Hammond. I'd say that's suggestive.'

'Or he'd fallen on hard times,' said Marcie, 'and he came back to his home town in the hope that one or two people would remember him kindly. Make that one person. He got lucky with an abandoned property, and changed his name to make the paperwork easier. I know you like neat packages, honey. I know you want the loose ends tied up. Life's a muddle. People do and say things for no good reason. Very little adds up. Give me the messy answer every time.'

'Sometimes things do add up,' I said. 'Otherwise the world wouldn't have got this far.'

'How far is that?'

We danced around the issue for a few days. I reckoned I'd got the answer; Marcie didn't think there was a question. As I saw it, Franky knew what he was doing when he first came back to town. He'd come back to claim his inheritance. When he changed his name to Hammond, he was taking his father's name, as you would, or at least as you might. Open-and-shut case, if you ask me.

Marcie wasn't impressed.

'It's like it was with Nelson and the money,' she said. 'You start with a preconception for which there's no evidence, and then you add this assumption and that assumption, till it sounds like the most reasonable proposition in the world. You can be as logical as you like, but if your starting point is screwed, so is the rest of it.'

I decided there was one way of finding out, and that was to ask Franky. Marcie didn't think that would work. She said Franky would deny it, and we wouldn't know whether he was lying or not. I decided to ask anyway, but wasn't sure when I'd get the chance. Since he'd occupied Mr Hammond's house, and since Arlene had occupied him, he was in the bar less often. But, as it happened, he dropped in for a meal one lunchtime, and I was there. We waited till his knife was about to plunge into his burger. Then I accosted him.

'When did you discover that Mr Hammond was your dad?'

'Huh?'

'Well, he was, wasn't he? That's why you came back

to town, Franky. That's why you're living in his house. That's why you've taken his name.'

Franky looked at me, then at Marcie, then at me again and shook his head. 'What are you on about?' he said. 'You know who my parents were.' He looked at Marcie again. 'You put him up to this, didn't you?'

'No, I did not,' said Marcie.

'Just because . . .' said Franky. 'Just because of – well, you know perfectly well what because of, Marcie – you think you can invent things about me.'

'I'm not inventing anything about you, Franky,' said Marcie. 'And I haven't said Mr Hammond was your father.'

Franky looked at me. 'So why should you think he was? Since when have you started having your own opinions?' That was below the belt.

'Mr Hammond left you the house in his will, didn't he?' I was winging it now.

'I'm not going there,' said Franky.

'Going where?'

'Anywhere you're going.' We looked at him, and he looked at us, and nobody said anything. Franky addressed his lunch. 'Look,' he said, one mouthful into his burger, 'all sorts of stuff's happened at one time or another. Before I left. After I'd left. Since I've been back. And to you too, I'm sure. And to everyone. It's gone, done and finished. I'm making it sound like a big deal. It's not a big deal, and it's not a little deal. It's . . . well, it's what it is.

Anyhow, it's done. We're not starting from there. We're starting from here.'

'I've no idea what you're talking about,' I said.

'Good,' said Franky. 'I'll be getting on with my meal, then.'

When the last customer had left, and the dishes and glasses had been cleared, Marcie joined me in the living room. We put our feet on the table.

'Well?' she asked.

'A draw, I reckon. What do you think?'

'I'm not sure. Perhaps you were right. I didn't expect him to be so defensive.'

I paused for a moment. 'What are you supposed to know, Marcie?'

'What do you mean?'

'When Franky turned to you and said, "You know perfectly well," what was he referring to?'

'I've no idea,' said Marcie. 'Are you sure he said that?'

'Oh, come on, you must have heard him.'

'Let's give it a rest, honey. I think we're both getting too wound up.'

That's the trouble with situations like this. The more you know, the less you know. You learn something, and you think, oh that's good, that's going to make things clearer, and it does no such thing. Maybe, with Franky, I was on the wrong track. As for what Marcie knew, she must have heard what Franky said. What was she hiding from me?

204

Until this point, Marcie and I had not seen the improvements that Franky had made to his new residence. The house had been occupied with our collusion, yet Franky hadn't invited us to look over the place. Now, a few days after our conversation in the bar, he asked me round to look at 'my house', as he'd taken to calling it. He invited me for one lunchtime, which must have been deliberate, so Marcie couldn't come.

Franky had continued to leave his car in our lot, around the corner, hidden from the road by our building. He still didn't want anyone to know where he was living, if it could be avoided, and we remained conspirators in the secret, although we'd said we didn't want to be. To anyone who passed the property on the road, with its big iron gates, the estate looked as derelict as ever. I walked in through the hole in the wire that I had first created, and which Franky had now expanded.

Considering it was little more than two months since Franky and Davy and I had clambered through the fence, the transformation to the house was amazing. What had been spent on it was time more than money, but it looked pretty darned good. Franky was a fine handyman, no question of it. We sat in the front room, on chairs he'd reclaimed from somewhere or other, with bottles of beer in our hands.

Everything about the visit was deliberate. That was evident when he invited me over, and it became more evident with each minute. I didn't associate Franky with deliberation. His excuse as a kid was that everything that happened to him happened by accident. He blundered around in other people's lives and, gee, how was he meant to know that this or that would be the consequence. That was how he got forgiven, by those who did forgive him. He'd grow up one day, people said. So had he now grown up, or had he always been premeditated, as Marcie believed?

'Hasn't changed much, this town, has it?' he said.

'No. That's what I like about it.'

'Me too, I suppose. Most of the time.'

'Are you planning to stay?'

'Yup. You're stuck with me now.'

'That's all right,' I said.

'Does Marcie feel the same way?'

'Why don't you ask her yourself?'

'That's kind of difficult.'

'Look, Franky, I don't know what there is between you and Marcie. There's something. What is it?'

'She doesn't like me,' said Franky.

'I know that, but it's not the whole story. You hint at it, and she hints at it, and neither of you will say what it is.'

'Do you really want to know?'

Did I want to know? I assumed I wanted to know. It's the sort of question to which you say yes without thinking. The fact that Franky asked it made me suspicious. Maybe I shouldn't want to know.

'What do you think?'

'Let me level with you,' said Franky.

That was a bad start. The last person who said that to me took me for a hundred bucks. That was also Franky, come to think of it, thirty years earlier. He'd be saying he believed in being honest with people next. If he didn't already have a reputation for unreliability, he'd have it now, as far as I was concerned.

'I'm not a natural recluse,' he went on.

'I know that.'

'Yet I find myself in this strange position. I want to see people here, and have a drink with them, but I don't want them to know where I live. You and Marcie, and Davy, and Arlene, are the only people I've been able to talk to. And now Davy has gone.'

'You seem to have plenty of Arlene,' I said. 'That should be some consolation.'

'Marcie told me a lie,' said Franky. 'She said she'd told Arlene where I was living. You were there. Remember?'

I said nothing.

'I nearly put my foot in it with Arlene. I was getting on to the subject, on the assumption that she knew, when it occurred to me that perhaps she didn't. That's the shit sort of way Marcie behaves toward me.'

'I don't understand, Franky. Arlene must know you're living here by now.'

'No, she doesn't.'

'Where do you go at nights?'

'None of your business,' said Franky.

'Why won't you tell her where you're living?'

'That's none of your business either. I need you to be discreet.'

'We are.'

'I wish I could be sure of that.'

'What does that mean?'

'In answer to your original question,' said Franky, 'I think, in the circumstances, you don't want to know what there is between me and Marcie.'

That settled it. Now I did want to know.

'I think I do, Franky. Tell me.'

'Why don't you get Marcie to tell you?'

'Because she won't. She won't admit that there's anything to tell.'

'Perhaps we should leave things that way,' said Franky.

'No, we shouldn't. It's too late for that now. Tell me.'

Franky had got me to the point where I was begging him to tell me, against his better judgement. If it back-fired – and this had all the hallmarks of a situation waiting to backfire – it would be my fault for making him tell me.

'Years ago,' said Franky, 'a little time before I left town, Marcie made a pass at me.'

'I thought you and she didn't get on.'

'We didn't. She came on to me real strong, all the same.'

'And?'

'And nothing. It was just the once. I didn't take it further.'

'So, Marcie made a pass at you. Once. Big deal. Why is it still eating both of you?'

'You know how I had to leave town because I'd got a girl pregnant?'

'Yeah.'

'Bullshit. Total bullshit. The rumours were started by Marcie, to pay me back for turning her down.'

'I don't believe you.'

'Which girl did I get pregnant?'

'I don't know. As I remember it, no one knew for certain.'

'Not good enough. There weren't many of us in our group, were there? How many girls? Ten? Twelve? I bet we could both still name them all. Not enough to make it easy to keep secrets. So. Tell me. Who did I get pregnant?'

'It's not difficult to keep quiet,' I said. 'Especially when there are reputations to protect.'

'What about my reputation? Nobody protected that. My reputation got shredded. That's why I had to leave town. Darned right, no one knew who the girl was. That's because there wasn't one.'

'Franky, it wasn't just those rumours that made life tough for you. You weren't popular with everyone. You got people to do things for you, and you didn't do anything for them. You borrowed money from people and didn't pay them back. In fact, you owe me a hundred bucks.' I deliberated whether to mention the three grand that had gone missing. 'Maybe more,' I added, without being specific.

'I'll pay you back if that's the problem,' said Franky. 'Look. Be reasonable. I was young.'

'We were all young. And we didn't all behave like you did.'

'So you don't believe me.'

'I don't see that it matters whether I believe you or not.'

'Of course it does,' said Franky. 'It matters because Marcie knows I'm living here and I don't trust her not to tell people.'

'What's that got to do with whether I believe you?'

'You're her husband. You can tell her you know what happened, starting those rumours about me. You can tell her you know why she started them. That should shut her up.'

'But I don't know.'

'I knew it was a mistake to tell you this,' said Franky. 'You're a good guy. You've always been a good guy. But you're weak as piss.'

'Thanks.'

'I guess I'll have to hope for the best, seeing that you're not going to help.'

'If your story's true, why should Marcie bear a grudge

all these years later? She's probably glad you turned her down.' That was me hoping what I said was true.

'You've seen how she behaves with me. It's a type of flirtation, wouldn't you say? Don't worry. I'll say no again, if the question arises.'

'You can be a real bastard, Franky. Everybody used to say you were, and they were right.'

'I tell it like it is. People don't want to hear that.'

'What I don't understand,' I said, 'is why you choose to live in this house when you don't want anyone to know you're here, and when Marcie lives next door.'

'It's complicated,' he said, and wouldn't say more.

Marcie was resting, feet on the table, when I got back to the house. I sat down next to her.

'So what's today's bullshit?' she asked.

'I don't know that it's bullshit,' I said. 'It might be true.'

'If it's Franky Albertino, it's bullshit.'

'He said you made a pass at him before he left town, all those years ago.'

'He said what?'

'That you made a pass at him.'

Marcie said nothing.

'You didn't make a pass at him?'

'Yes,' she said. 'I did.'

'What happened then?'

'Nothing happened then. Franky wasn't interested in me.'

I didn't say anything for a moment. I was trying to work out how some trivial event, several decades earlier, still exercised such a hold over Marcie. I expect I made passes at loads of girls at that age. I couldn't even tell you their names now. All right, girls didn't so often make passes at boys in those days, but it wasn't unknown. I found it hard to escape the conclusion that Marcie had been infatuated with Franky then, that she was infatuated with him now, and that she was covering it up with hostility.

'Why does it still matter?' I asked.

'Because I'm ashamed of it. I don't think I have much to be ashamed of in my life, but I'm ashamed of that. Always have been.'

'But it's such a minor thing,' I said.

'What troubled me,' said Marcie, 'was that I could never figure out why I did it. I didn't like Franky. I didn't trust Franky. So why would I fancy Franky? It made me doubt my own judgement. It made me uncertain who I was.'

'Do you still fancy him?'

'You've got to be joking.'

'Well, that's a relief,' I said. Marcie didn't smile. 'So, when he pitched up a few months ago, what were you feeling?'

'Horrified. It brought back all the shame. I was counting on never seeing Franky again. I thought I'd put it all behind me.'

'How old were you when it happened?'

'I don't know,' said Marcie. 'About nineteen, perhaps. It wasn't long before I started dating you.'

'Why didn't you ever tell me this, honey?'

'It wasn't your problem,' said Marcie. 'It was between me and Franky. And I felt ashamed, like I said. And Franky was your friend. It felt like a betrayal.'

'But it wasn't. We weren't dating then, you said.'

'No. I know.' Marcie sighed. 'Let's just leave it there, shall we?'

'Sure.'

I didn't have much choice but to leave it there. I didn't want to leave it, but there was no point in pursuing it. I had asked questions, of Franky and of Marcie, and I'd got answers. The answers tallied. I could believe that Marcie was ashamed of what she did at the time. And embarrassed, probably. Perhaps humiliated. What I found harder to believe were her feelings all these years later.

Marcie couldn't stand Franky. That was beyond doubt. But she was not indifferent to him, nor he to her. Love and hate aren't strangers to each other. Marcie might dislike Franky; that didn't mean she wasn't attracted to him. I felt that the ball of string was still unravelling.

13

One Sunday evening in late October, soon after these conversations, Marcie and I took a walk through the streets of town. We did that from time to time, especially on a Sunday. It was our day off, and Steve was left in sole charge until the evening. We had another reason to take that walk now: we wanted to take a look at 7 Pine Street, the address that Arlene had scribbled on the back of her shopping list.

It had been one of those dead and bluesy days, a day for half living. With the evening had come a fog. That was weird. We almost never get fog round here. Maybe the moon was blue, if we'd been able to see it.

The fog was thick: not thick enough, when we started walking, to blanket houses, to erase landmarks, but thick enough to render them in outline only, to take away what was familiar, and leave them as husks of something or other, I'm not sure what. It was the first cold night of the season. Our breaths steamed ahead of us, mingling with the fog, as if the fog was the cumulative total of the town's breath that day. As if the purpose of life had been to cloak ourselves and each other in the fogs of our own breathing.

'Is this Cross Street?' asked Marcie.

'I'd say so.'

I think it was Cross Street. It could have been McKinley, or Main even. Not the shopping bit of Main, but some bit. Streets that had been intimate to us since birth, that were discrete arteries in the body of which we were a part, fused that night into each other, losing shape, coherence, and a solid identity. We walked them as strangers, attempting to make out what we could not see, wanting to impose an order on the amorphous objects that presented themselves and then withdrew, like giant squids rolling their way across the ocean floor. Trying to take what had long been familiar and to make it familiar again. No one else thought it was much of a night for being out and about. We didn't pass a soul.

'We haven't seen much of Arlene recently,' I said. 'She's hardly been in since she took up with Franky. I miss her.'

'What is there to miss?'

'I thought you liked her.'

'I do,' said Marcie. 'But I get tired of people who appear to have depths and who never reveal them. I want to know what's there. I suspect it's usually things they haven't managed to resolve yet, and never will. Still, at least it means we don't see much of Franky.'

'You sure have a down on him, don't you?' I said.

'To me, the astonishing thing is that you don't. Despite the fact that he's stolen three grand of our money. Nothing seems to alter your opinion of Franky.'

'We don't know he stole our money.'

'Oh, for goodness' sake,' said Marcie.

'Some opinions got set a long, long time ago,' I said. 'They're beyond changing. I'm sorry, but I can't help it.'

'Forget it,' said Marcie. 'Franky's not going to come between us. Just don't expect me to share your opinion. I suppose one day we'll be shot of him.'

Marcie came to an abrupt halt, so I did the same.

'What's up?'

'I thought I was about to walk into a tree,' said Marcie. 'Is that a tree there?'

'I don't know. I'll take a look.' I groped my way forward, arms stretching out and sideways. 'I don't think there's a tree,' I said. 'I haven't found one yet.'

'Where are you?'

'I'm here.'

'Where's here?'

Now I went off looking for Marcie, as I'd looked for the tree, arms spread to find her, like it was a game of blind man's bluff. And she did the same to find me, and we called out names and tried to judge if the voice of the other sounded near or distant. After a while, I felt a hand touch my waist and, after we'd grappled around a bit, and ascertained that we had indeed found each other, we paused, arms round shoulders.

'You take me to the nicest places,' said Marcie.

'It's got a lot worse. How the hell are we going to find our way to Pine?'

'Never mind Pine. How are we going to find our way home? Where do you think we are?'

'There's a neon sign winking over there,' I said. 'Let's take a look.' I held Marcie's hand tightly and we made for the light like two stray moths.

'What on earth are you doing now?' Marcie asked. I was dancing a jig on the sidewalk, so you couldn't blame her.

'This is Micky's gas station,' I said. 'So we're on the corner of Pine. Would you believe it? What a fantastic piece of navigation on my part. Right up there with Christopher Columbus.'

'Columbus didn't know where he was going either,' said Marcie.

'The trouble is,' I said, 'I don't know if there's much point in going further. We won't be able to see Mrs Riessen's house, assuming we can find it.'

'There's every point. Now we've got a pretext to knock on her door and say we're lost.'

'We can't do that.'

'Why not? We'll never get a better chance.'

'She'll think we're nuts.'

'We are,' said Marcie. 'Which way do the numbers run on Pine?'

'I've no idea. I guess it's odd numbers one side and evens the other.'

We started with the first house on the left. We groped around looking for a number on the mailbox or some-where; couldn't see a thing.

'Have you got your lighter on you?' asked Marcie.

'I've given up the cigars, like I told you.'

'Have you got your lighter on you?'

I rummaged in my coat pocket. 'Oh, yes,' I said. 'It seems I have. That's lucky.'

Marcie snorted. At least we could now see the number, and it was number 1. We counted up three driveways and checked again. Number 5, for some reason.

'Close, but no cigar,' said Marcie.

'I'm glad we're not looking for number 87.'

The next driveway belonged to number 7. We didn't see the lights from the front room until we were five feet from the house. We walked up to the front door. I flicked the lighter again and saw a plaque with the name of Riessen. I rang the bell.

The woman who answered the door was, on aver-age, in her mid-sixties. That is to say, I thought she was around sixty and Marcie thought she was around sev-enty. She peered at us suspiciously, as well she might. I explained who we were, and what had happened, and asked if I could use the phone. I rang Steve to tell him we wouldn't be back for a while. Steve said we weren't missing much. The place was empty except for Mike and

Franky. Our involuntary hostess said we could stay for a while until the fog eased off.

While I was waiting for Steve to answer the phone, I surveyed the room and the word that came to mind was comfortable. Everything was comfortable. None of the contents was showy, but none of them would have come cheap. Next to the telephone was a silver frame with the photo of a distinguished-looking man with a pencil moustache. I looked at it in an absent-minded way. And then I looked again. Darn me if it wasn't Jack Nightingale. There was another photo of him on the wall, kitted out in the strip of the Pittsburgh Steelers.

But for the fact that this woman was called Riessen, I would have said we were in Jack's home and this was his wife, or more likely his widow. However, Jack had said he lived in the bastard town next door and was divorced. He used to show up in the bar with a redhead on his arm sometimes. A variety of redheads, in fact: he said he had a thing about them. Our hostess looked like she'd been ginger once. It could have made sense if she'd married a Mr Riessen after she'd married Jack, and Jack had then moved to the bastard town. If that had happened, why would she have pictures of her first husband on display? I looked at the photos, and then at Marcie. Marcie looked at me, and then at the photos. There needed to be a question. The difficulty was how to phrase it.

'It's strange,' said Marcie. 'The man in the photo by the telephone looks like someone we used to know.'

219

'Jack Nightingale,' I said. 'Marcie and I have a bar on the other side of town. Jack used to drop in from time to time.'

'Oh, no,' said the woman I wanted to call Mrs Nightingale. 'You must be mistaken. The photo is of my late husband, Jack Riessen. He passed on three years ago.'

'I'm so sorry,' said Marcie.

'And he was teetotal,' said the woman I now needed to call Mrs Riessen. 'As am I. We wouldn't think of going into a drinking establishment.'

If this had indeed been Jack Nightingale's home, it was now apparent why he didn't spend much time here. While in the bar, he would consume legendary quantities of bourbon. I wasn't sure where to take the conversation, assuming I should be trying to take it anywhere.

'We must be mistaken,' I said.

'People often resemble other people, don't they?' said Mrs Riessen. She didn't seem put out. 'It can make life very complicated.'

Especially if you're Jack Nightingale doubling up as Jack Riessen, I thought.

'It can indeed,' I said.

'Funnily enough,' said Marcie, 'a little while ago, a woman came into our bar, asking the way to Pine. She was looking for Jack Nightingale.'

That was brilliant on Marcie's part. I nearly believed her myself. In fact, I was close to saying, 'You never told me that.' Mrs Riessen did not react. Not a flicker. If

Arlene had come to look for this house, she'd failed to find its occupant. Or failed to mention that she was looking for Jack.

'What was Mr Riessen's line of business?' I asked.

'He was a paper merchant,' said Mrs Riessen. 'The business took him all over the place. Jack worked like the devil, poor man. He was hardly ever at home. It's what killed him so young, in my opinion.'

'His death must have come as a great shock,' said Marcie.

'It most certainly did. And it was several days before I found out. He was travelling at the time. He had a heart attack on the sidewalk. It was the fourth of July. Not the sort of Independence Day I'd imagined. Jack found the strength to stagger inside a nearby store. It was a liquor store, I was told. I think he would have appreciated the irony. He had a good sense of humour. He collapsed on the floor there.'

'Did the two of you have children?' I asked.

'No,' said Mrs Riessen. 'We didn't.' She rose from her chair, crossed to the window and parted the curtains. 'No, I don't have children. Do you?'

'We have children in Colorado,' said Marcie.

'Well, there we are. There we are.'

'I'm surprised we haven't met before,' said Marcie. 'It's strange how you can live in a small place for ages and not meet people.'

'Oh, I've not been here long,' said Mrs Riessen. 'I

221

moved here the year after Jack died, so about two years ago. We'd lived in Indiana before. I found I didn't want to stay there afterwards, and Jack had spoken highly of this town.'

'Do you like it here?'

'Yes. Yes, I think so. It suits me perfectly well. I'm not sure why Jack thought quite so much of it, though.'

There was a pause. Marcie took the risk of impertinence with her next question. 'At least it looks as though he left you well provided for,' she said.

'I suppose so,' said Mrs Riessen. 'Yes, I think so. I mean, I have everything I need. The lawyer explained it to me when Jack died. It was rather complicated and I don't think I took it in. What with Jack's death, and all sorts of people wanting to ask all sorts of questions, because, well, I don't know why. Because it's what they do, I suppose. It came as a shock. I don't think I understood very much of it. Jack's lawyer and accountant took care of everything for me.'

Mrs Riessen went to the window again and parted the curtains. It was difficult to know if she was expecting someone, or if she was seeing whether the fog had cleared so she could get rid of us. I wondered if she'd spent years of her life peeking between curtains at each sound of a car passing, each hint of a part-time husband returning, and now did it from habit, when there was no husband and no sound of cars.

'How does it look out there?' I asked.

'A bit better, I think. It's hard to tell. Yes, I think it's a bit better.'

'We'd best be on our way then. Thanks for the shelter.'

Marcie added her thanks and we shuffled crabwise through the front door, the three of us murmuring platitudes. Mrs Riessen was right: it was a bit better. Good enough to see where each new footstep was landing. Good enough to distinguish the road from the sidewalk.

'I don't know what the hell to make of that,' I said, as we walked the deserted streets home.

'Are you sure those photos were of Jack Nightingale? I know it looked like him, but could it have been someone else?'

'No,' I said. 'It was Jack. I knew it straightaway and so did you.'

'All right,' said Marcie. 'Next question. Do you remember what line of business Jack was in?'

'Not for certain. I thought it was stationery. Close enough to paper, I suppose. You'd think we should be able to remember more. How often did he come in, would you say? Must have been hundreds of times. Over what? Ten years at least.'

'Do you remember what car he drove?'

'No,' I said.

'Neither do I,' said Marcie. 'In fact, I don't remember him having a car.'

'He must have had a car. Everyone comes to us in a car.'

'Unless they're like Franky,' said Marcie, 'and live next door.'

'You think Jack Nightingale was our neighbour? That he was Mr Hammond? As well as being Jack Riessen? That all those years he came into the bar he was just strolling through from next door?'

'No,' said Marcie. 'Not really.'

'It's not impossible, though. We wouldn't have known.'

'Lots of things aren't impossible,' said Marcie. 'Doesn't mean they're true. It's not likely that Jack Nightingale lived next door. We're trying to make a dozen things fit into one neat story. I don't buy it.'

'You never buy neat stories. Doesn't mean they aren't true.'

We walked on in silence for a while.

'There must have been other things we knew about Jack,' said Marcie.

'It's not a question of what we knew. It's a question of how much of it was true. He said he was divorced. False, it now seems. He said he lived in that bastard town along the river. False. He said he supported the Cleveland Browns. False.'

'How do you know that?'

'Because, in the photo on the wall, he was wearing the kit of the Steelers.' Marcie raised an eyebrow: we don't see eye to eye on the charms of football. 'They're from Pittsburgh. I'm sure Jack said lots of other things too. Who knows which of them were true?'

'You can lie and tell the truth at the same time,' said Marcie.

'I'm getting out of my depth here,' I said. 'Please explain.'

'You can tell the truth and give a misleading impression. Maybe it was true that Jack had been divorced. Then he remarried. Maybe he had homes all over the place, including in the town next door. It looks like he had money.'

'That would take a lot of money.'

'Perhaps he had a lot of money,' said Marcie.

'What did you make of Mrs Riessen? Or Mrs Nightingale, if you prefer. Was she as ignorant as she appeared?'

'I think she knows more about the personal side than she's letting on,' said Marcie. 'No. That's the wrong way of putting it. I think she suspects things she doesn't know.'

'Such as?'

'I think she believes Jack may have had children.'

'How come?'

'It was the way she answered the question about children. The emphasis made it sound as if children fitted into the equation somehow, but they weren't hers. Of course, if Jack had been married before, that would make sense.'

'She sure as hell seemed confused about the money side of things,' I said. 'No doubt the lawyer and accountant dealt with that, and I bet they were crooks. Someone

225

was needed to pull the pieces together for some people, and to stop them being pulled together for others. Jack would have seen to that.'

'I wonder where he died,' said Marcie.

'Who knows? Could have been anywhere. Might have been the bastard town.'

'Wherever it was,' said Marcie, 'there would need to have been two sets of people to identify the body, two places where that had to happen, two stories to put out, and two burials, one of them with an empty coffin. No wonder it took several days for her to hear about it.'

'Jesus,' I said. 'What a mess. The funeral parlour must have been in on it. They must have carted Jack's body from one place to the other for identification.'

'There's a bent world,' said Marcie, 'which honest people never see. Find one bent person and you find the rest. A bent lawyer can recommend you a bent accountant. A bent accountant can recommend you a bent funeral director.'

'You're making it sound like there's a freemasonry of corruption out there.'

'There is,' said Marcie.

'I wonder what ID Jack had on him when he died,' I said. 'I imagine a lot of shit came out that Mrs R didn't want to know about.'

'And still doesn't,' said Marcie. 'I expect the lawyer smoothed most of it out.'

We were getting close to home now, or I thought we

were. The fog had worsened again and we were losing our bearings.

'At least we know the Jack that Arlene's been looking for,' I said. 'Can't be a coincidence she had that address. I suppose she found something when she was rummaging in Indiana. Are we going to tell her?'

'No,' said Marcie. 'I don't think we should. She may already know, of course. If she doesn't, she should be left to find out for herself. We don't know what we're getting tangled up in here.'

'What do you reckon? Was Jack her father?'

'Who knows?' said Marcie. 'She doesn't look much like him.'

'That doesn't prove anything.'

'None of this proves anything,' said Marcie.

'Of course, we may be barking up the wrong tree altogether,' I said. 'This may have nothing to do with Arlene. It may be that Jack was telling the truth all along. It may be that Mrs R is some deranged woman who had a crush on him and has convinced herself she was married to him.'

'Now you're being ridiculous,' she said. I could sense her hands wanting to go to her hips for emphasis. It's hard to do that when you're walking, and they only made it halfway, like a still shot of John Wayne on the draw.

Was it ridiculous? Who knows? Most of the explanations seemed ridiculous in one way or another. I wasn't altogether sure that Jack was even dead. If you can have one empty coffin, why not two?

Since that evening, I've imagined myself living the life of an alter ego. I have dreams about it. I'm a realistic fantasist. There have to be some parts of the fantasy that are true, because I can then more easily imagine the parts that are not. So I don't dream of being Frank Sinatra or Jack Kennedy, because nothing in my life coincides with anything in theirs. My name is Greg Olsen and I live in Topeka, Kansas. I'm the principal of a high school and my wife is called Martha. We have six children, three girls and three boys. On our summer vacations, we go camping in a Winnebago. We don't go to Colorado.

I feel comfortable as Greg. He's more of an idealist than I am and doesn't make cynical comments. He was unfaithful to Martha some years back. He doesn't think Martha knows, but he's not sure and he beats himself up about it. He worries that he might not get to heaven. That's another difference between us. He's religious. I don't know why I made him religious. It means I need to worry about getting to heaven on his behalf, which is a waste of worry because I don't believe in heaven.

Could I be Greg Olsen, as well as being myself? Forget the practicalities, like the fact that barkeepers don't get to lead double lives. In principle, could I do it? Could I be living in Topeka with a wife called Martha, have become a teacher, like I did, have remained a teacher, like I didn't, and be expressing opinions that are similar to mine without being identical, and in a tone of voice that is different? Could I be living in Topeka, going to church on Sunday mornings with the family, and smiling at the pastor in a faithful way? Could I be doing the things that would make me Greg Olsen?

Only if I was Greg Olsen, I think. Otherwise, no; I couldn't. That is the difference between me and Jack Nightingale, assuming Jack did lead a double life. Anyone can dream it. Few can do it. The ones that do are different sorts of human being. Jack might have dreamt about it before he did it; he might not have done. He could have seen an opportunity, grabbed it and worked out the consequences later. Perhaps Jack kept as many things the same between his different lives as he could. His first name, for a start. It would have made the role playing easier if there was less to remember. In that case, Jack did not have an alter ego. He had a duplicate. There were two Jacks out there.

Except it would not have been like that. The places would have been different, and so would the wives or mistresses, so Jack would have been different. Different while being himself. That's what I'm trying to understand. Most of us present variable facets of ourselves to the world. None of us is solely the person we seem. There is more to us and there is other to us. Mass murderers are routinely described as 'very ordinary' by their neighbours. What we seem to be is equally an illusion whether we live one life or several. Perhaps we are all many people. That's what Arlene believes.

14

One grey afternoon at the end of October, soon after the visit to Mrs Riessen, I was in the bar room, clearing the remains of lunch away and arranging the place for the evening. It was the day Marcie went to her exercise class, so I was alone. There was a creak of the swing doors, and Franky's head poked through. He walked in, tentatively, looked around the room.

'Marcie not here?'

'No. It's her class today.'

'Oh, yeah. I'd forgotten that.'

'Did you want to see her?'

'No. No. It was you I wanted to see. Will she be back soon?'

'I doubt it,' I said. 'When she's done with exercising, she'll be picking up our Halloween costumes from town.'

'You're going to the parade?'

'Yes.'

'We're going too.'

'What as? Romeo and Juliet?'

'Could be,' said Franky. 'I don't know. Arlene's getting the costumes. It's a surprise.'

'Want a drink?'

'Thanks. I'll have a bourbon. A large one.'

I poured one for myself too. We took our drinks to a table.

'OK,' I said. 'Well, here we are and not likely to be interrupted. What do you want to talk about?'

'You know that Arlene's looking for someone called Jack?'

'I think everyone knows that.'

'Do you know who Jack is?'

'No,' I said. Franky was the last person I'd share the news with.

'Does Marcie know?'

'If she knew, I'd know,' I said. 'Why does it matter?'

'Did Arlene ever talk about a woman named Riessen to you?'

'No.'

'She mentioned her to me. She said Mrs Riessen lived up on Pine. She thought she'd got something to do with Jack. I don't know where she picked that up. Somewhere on her travels, I guess. Anyway, she's been to look at the house once or twice, but hasn't found the nerve to ring the bell.'

'That's news to me.'

'A week or two ago,' said Franky, 'Arlene asked if I'd help her find Jack. I said I would, because I could see it was important to her and I didn't want to say no. I hadn't a clue who Jack was, and I didn't see how I could help. I was just being supportive. Later, when she told me about Mrs Riessen, I suggested we should visit her house. I said I'd go with her if it would help. She didn't want to do that. I got the feeling that she wanted to approach the matter less directly. Not that she said that, of course. She clammed up on me as usual. So I let it go.'

'And then?'

'A few nights back I was in here. It must have been Sunday, because you weren't here. I had a long conversation with Mike. I wanted to find out why Nelson wasn't around anymore. It's not that I liked him especially, but he was in here almost every night and then suddenly he wasn't. I was curious.'

'Did Mike tell you?'

'No. He looked shifty. I think he knew all right. He just wasn't saying. I'm sure you know too, and you won't tell me either.'

I said nothing.

'No,' said Franky. 'I thought not. Anyway, that's beside the point. Mike and I got talking about the other regulars here over the years. I knew some of them, of course, back from when I was in town before. Like I knew Mike himself, in fact. He started telling me about someone called Jack Nightingale. Remember him?'

'No one could forget Jack Nightingale. He was quite a character.'

'So I hear. Mike said he stopped coming. Again suddenly. About five years ago. Is that right?'

'Yes.'

'And it was about five years ago?'

'Yes,' I said. 'About that.'

'Not three years ago?'

'I don't think so,' I said. 'Three years. Five years. What does it matter?'

'It probably doesn't,' said Franky. 'Do you know what happened to him?'

'No, I don't. We assumed he'd died. We don't know that. You're making it sound like a mystery, but it's not. It's one of the downsides of the job. People stop coming and we don't know why.'

'Unless they're Nelson,' said Franky. I didn't smile. 'Do you think it's possible,' he went on, 'that Jack Nightingale is or was the Jack that Arlene's looking for? That thought must have occurred to you.'

'Yes,' I said. 'It's occurred to me. But I've no reason to think it's him. Arlene said it wasn't when she first came in.'

'That was a long time ago. Things may have changed.' Franky looked at his glass, then straight at me. 'Life's hard enough to understand when people share the information they've got,' he said. 'When they don't, it's impossible.'

'What's that supposed to mean?'

'There's stuff you know that you're not telling. Ditto Arlene. Ditto Marcie. Ditto me, if it comes to that. And ditto plenty of other people, I expect. If we pooled what we knew, we'd be wiser. None of us are into collaborative ventures, it would appear.'

'What's eating you?' I asked. 'You seem really worked up over Jack. Not like you to worry about someone else's problem. Why else are you here?'

Franky smiled. 'Once I could have said, "No other reason," to you, and you'd have believed me.'

'I don't automatically believe anything you say now, Franky. I seem to remember Henry Ford saying he knew half his advertising budget was wasted, but he didn't know which half. I feel much the same with you and the truth. Half of what you say is bullshit, but I don't know which half.'

'I think I do better than half.'

'In which direction?'

'The reason I'm here,' said Franky, 'is that I'm about to propose to Arlene. That's between the two of us. I'm asking her tomorrow, at Halloween. Arlene's been looking forward to Halloween for weeks. She never went to a parade when she was a kid. I want to make it a really special day for her.'

'Congratulations,' I said. 'I hope the two of you are happy.'

'You might sound as though you mean it.'

'Where do you intend to live?'

'Where do you think? Next door.'

'Does Arlene know that?'

'Not yet. That's a surprise for later in the week.'

'Well, it's all very interesting to know,' I said, a little sourly. 'But it still doesn't explain why you're here.'

'Our lives are about to change,' said Franky. 'I don't want any baggage from the past cluttering up the future. The biggest piece of baggage is Jack. Arlene is obsessed with Jack. She travels to different places to look for him. She gets sent three or four local newspapers each week. You don't get to see any of that. It's what goes on when Arlene's not at the bar. I want to solve the mystery once and for all because, until it is solved, there won't be any peace for her or for me. I'd hoped you could help me. It seems that you can't. Or won't.'

'I'm sorry,' I said. 'Not my problem. I expect you'll understand that.'

He looked slowly around the bar. 'Perhaps it was a mistake to have come back,' he said.

'That's what Marcie said when you arrived.'

'She was right. Clever old Marcie. Still, I wouldn't have met Arlene otherwise.' Franky paused. 'I suppose you told Marcie what I told you in the house.'

'Yes,' I said. 'She confirmed what you said.'

'Good,' said Franky. 'That's one thing cleared up.'

We sat in silence for a while. I didn't know what Franky was thinking. I was trying to decide whether to ask him a particular question. I thought I might know the answer and, if I was right, I wouldn't ever want to see Franky again, even if he was living next door. No great problem, you could say. I never saw Mr Hammond for decades; no reason I'd have to see Franky. Except I'd always know he was there.

'I wouldn't say it was cleared up,' I said. 'It's only cleared up if I believe what you both told me, and I'm not sure that I do. So let me ask you a direct question. Did you get Marcie pregnant?'

'What the hell makes you think that?'

'Answer the question, Franky.'

He said nothing for a long time. Just sat there shaking his head.

'I can't answer it,' he said.

'Why not? It's a straight question. Give me a straight answer.'

'I can't. I never wanted to discuss this. Remember? I said that you shouldn't want to know about it. You should have listened. What's Marcie been saying to you?'

Marcie hadn't said anything about a pregnancy. A number of thoughts had been rattling around my mind and, although they didn't amount to more than a perhaps, they were disconcerting enough to make me dare to ask the question.

The rumour that Franky had got a girl pregnant had faded over the years, but it had never disappeared. I'd heard it repeated a few times in the previous months. At the time, it had seemed to be more than a rumour, close to an accepted fact. It didn't circulate only through the young men in our crowd, telling salacious tales about things they would never laugh at now, especially if their daughters were involved. It came from several of the girls too, and they seemed sure of it.

Then there was the ambiguity over what had happened between Marcie and Franky. Both said that nothing had happened, or very little, but I still couldn't fathom why a non-event should produce such strong emotions all these years later.

Finally, there was what had happened when Marcie and I started dating. I elided time when I mentioned that earlier; made it sound as if one day we took up with each other and after that we were a permanent item. It didn't happen quite that way. We did begin dating suddenly, unexpectedly even, despite having known each other for many years. For the first two months or so, we were inseparable. Marcie was living at home, on the family farm, ten miles out of town, and working in the haberdasher's store. She'd come in by bus in the morning. Most evenings, when she'd finished work and I'd finished my teacher training, we'd do things together. If she missed the last bus, I'd drive her home.

One evening, we were due to go to the pictures and I'd arranged to meet her at the store. She wasn't there. I'd arrived just before closing time, and the manageress told me that Marcie had been taken seriously ill and wouldn't be in for some while. In fact, she made it sound as if she mightn't be back at all. Alarmed, I ran home and telephoned the farm. I must have sounded agitated.

I couldn't speak to Marcie. I spoke to her mom, who confirmed what I'd been told. Her mom sounded agitated too. No one knew what the problem was, she said. The doctors were working on it, and in the meantime Marcie had to stay at home and couldn't see anyone. She was at home for four or five months in the end. I never saw her in that time, and I never got to find out what her illness was. 'Women's problems,' was all her mom said. I didn't see why that should stop me seeing her. It's not like she was contagious.

Marcie didn't say even that much. We talked on the phone, almost every night. What I most remember was her pleading with me not to abandon her. Not that I had any intention of that. She seemed desperate that I should believe it was no reflection on me, that she loved me very much and that, as soon as she was better, we would be together again, wouldn't we?

Which we were. And we didn't talk about it then, and we haven't talked about it since. To start with, Marcie said it was too painful to discuss. She was so fragile and tearful at the time, and so grateful to me for sticking by her, that I didn't like to press her. Over time, I got used to the idea that it never would be discussed. Of course I wondered, and of course it was peculiar. I don't think I ever thought it suspicious, at least as it affected me, until recent weeks, when I started reflecting on Franky's past, and on those old rumours.

I also remembered that it was while Marcie was ill

that Franky left town. I remember that because, when she was no longer there to have fun with, I spent a lot more time with the boys, and I was looking forward to spending more time with Franky. He didn't hang around very long. It must have been soon after Marcie took to her bed that Franky took to his heels.

All these remembrances were what gave me the courage to ask Franky the question. I told them to him now, or most of them.

'Until the other day, I never knew how much you knew,' said Franky. 'I couldn't know what Marcie had told you. That's why I've been a bit defensive when Marcie's around. It's why I hesitated before telling you what there'd been between us. I was trying to work out what you already knew. When we were at the house, I decided you didn't know very much, so I told you some of it.'

'You lied.'

'To spare you,' said Franky.

'Of course. Like always.'

'Don't be like that. You're saying I should have told you the truth. I'm telling you I don't know what the truth is.'

'Your refusal to answer the question is telling me,' I said.

'That's not fair,' said Franky. 'I'll tell you what I know. All of it. It's true that Marcie made a pass at me. It's not true that I didn't respond. I did respond. We made love that evening. It was the only time it happened, but it happened. It's also true that Marcie got pregnant. As to who the father was, I can't tell you.'

'Who else could it have been?'

Franky took a breath. 'Several of the girls we knew were flirts, weren't they? Some of them were outrageous flirts. Marcie wasn't one of those, as you know. But she was a flirt all the same, only more discreet. I could name you two other guys for certain who had a fling with her at the same time. Any of us could have been the father.'

'Who were they?'

'I'm not telling you that, full stop,' said Franky. 'One of them is still in town.'

'How come you got to know about the other two?'

'They wanted to brag, and they bragged to me. Guys always wanted to brag to me. I don't know why. I suppose they thought it would bring them kudos. You did it too, if you remember. Then, when we heard rumours that Marcie was pregnant, the three of us discussed it and we agreed we'd keep quiet.'

'The rumours all concerned you.'

'All rumours concerned me. They still do. That's what I'm complaining about. Anything goes wrong, and it's let's-blame-Franky time.'

We sat there, glaring at each other.

'The funny thing,' he said after a while, 'is that I've never had kids. None that I know of for definite. I'd have liked kids. I'm hoping to have kids with Arlene.'

He paused. 'Marcie must have kept the baby, don't you think? If she'd had an abortion, she wouldn't have been at home all that time. Four or five months, did you say?'

'About that.'

'I don't suppose you know if it was a boy or a girl?'

'How would I?'

'No, of course.' He reflected for a moment. 'Did you happen to notice if Marcie had a much younger brother or sister around the place?'

'No,' I said. 'And I think I would have noticed.'

'In that case,' said Franky, 'I guess the baby was adopted.'

'I suppose so.'

'I've heard it said that farming families try to keep these things within the community. They don't like anonymous adoptions, through an agency in town. They prefer to find a couple locally who don't have kids of their own. That's what I've been told.'

'Franky,' I said, 'if I ever hear that you've gone nosing around the neighbourhood farms asking questions, I'll skin you alive.'

'I won't,' said Franky. 'But the kid might want to know who its natural father is. I would.'

I bit my tongue at that. 'Perhaps the kid will want to know who its natural mother is,' I said.

'Perhaps the kid already does,' said Franky. 'Perhaps they see each other.'

I wanted him gone now. There was no more to be

said, so we didn't say it. Franky got up. He shook my hand and then walked slowly through the doors, outbound.

My first feeling when he left the room concerned the enormity of what he had told me. I didn't ask myself whether I believed him, which is normally the first question when Franky tells you something. I had got most of the way to the answer myself and Franky had pushed me over the line. There would be issues for me to deal with. Most of all, the equality that the deaths of Bobby and Roseanne had bestowed on Marcie and me. Marcie still had a child, or she probably did, and I did not. But how hard for her to lose those two and then not be able to raise the one that remained.

Since Franky's return, things between Marcie and me had changed. How could they not have done? Even before knowing what I knew now, things had changed. We hadn't discussed how Franky's reappearance was affecting us. Partly, on my side, for fear of life unravelling again; partly because there was nothing to be done about it, and discussion seemed futile. For the past few months, Marcie had been forced to share time in the bar with someone who might have been the father of her child. Someone she had thought never to see again. Someone who was now our neighbour. No wonder matters were strained and unnatural between the two of them.

I didn't debate with myself whether to tell Marcie what I'd been told. This was a time for lashing the boat to its moorings, not for rocking it. Besides, she had made the decision not to entangle me many years ago, and she'd stuck by it, even at times when it must have been difficult. I felt I should respect her decision. Whether it had been the right decision was another matter, but once made, it was made.

Some women might be able to obliterate such a memory. I don't think that Marcie's one of them. She will have carried it with her, will always be carrying it. It was possible she did see her child sometimes. Trust Franky to suggest that, to twist the knife further when it was already plunged deep.

My next feeling was one of horror that Franky would now be our long-term neighbour. The fact that Arlene would be with him made it worse in a way. I shouldn't have been surprised when he first came back. For all the big talk, all the bravado, Franky was a small town boy, like me. When he was young, he gave the impression of someone who wanted to take the world by storm. He hadn't. I continued to believe he was Hammond's son, and in that case the immediate impulse for his return had been his father's death and the house. I felt he wanted to come back in any event. The bigger world was too scary. This place was his backyard and his comfort zone.

Maybe I should have told him about Riessen and Nightingale, but I was wary of getting drawn too deeply into Franky's world. I could defend him to Marcie, if I needed to, but I was finding it difficult to defend him to myself any longer. I wanted shot of him, and shot of all the entanglements that came with him. I would have to ban him from the bar, close him out of my mind and pretend he wasn't living a few yards away. Marcie would somehow have to find a way of doing the same.

We would deal with this, because we would have to deal with it. I felt relief that I now knew what had happened to Marcie during those four or five months. One day, I would be stronger for all this, and Marcie and I would be stronger together.

I felt the churning of oceans begin to flood back into my life.

We had chosen to row upon tideless waters, Marcie and me. It was a choice made years ago. We made it together without discussing it much. With near wordless consent, we had rejected the turbulence of whirlpool and eddy, the undertow of strangling weeds and uncertain forces. By a sheltered pool we had rested. It was not too late for us to have had other children. We didn't want to take that risk. We needed certainty, and there was no certainty.

It's true that I did want to have a bar. I also wanted to do other things, and so did Marcie, and I think we would have done them, but for, but for. Something froze after that. To stick where you are is as much of a gamble as to move on, only it doesn't feel that way, so we stuck where we were. As things have turned out, it hasn't proved much of a gamble. I shouldn't be saying things like this. I'm talking like an old man. I'm not much past fifty. There may be a way to go yet.

Let's be positive. There is a way to go. It's not too late to sample another life, to become slightly different people. The question is whether we can muster the strength to do it. We carry a load of baggage around with us. It is shared between us, but a weight on both our shoulders. It would feel like a betrayal to dump it, and I don't know if we could. Unless we do, we're not going anywhere.

We could sell up and I was beginning to feel that we should. I get offers from time to time, and some of them are tempting. Nothing holds us to this town except memories and the bar, and the memories are now sour. It has never seemed to be the right time to do it. We're too young to be doing nothing; too old to be learning new ways. It's a young world these days. But maybe this is now the right time.

What I need to do first is to go to Colorado. I should go to Colorado with Marcie. Not to stay there, but at least to go. It's been my choice not to do that, and it's out of cowardice. Marcie has been braver. The longer I leave it, the harder it gets. At the moment, it feels impossible. However, it's not impossible and it should be done. If that can be achieved, who knows what else might be achieved, and will be achieved, and what rutted cart tracks might be smoothed.

The swing doors swung again and Marcie walked in, face pink from exercise and arms laden with parcels. I gave her a hug, in so much as I could reach her. We smiled.

'Wait till you see this,' she said. 'Boy, are we going to stand out tomorrow night.' She started unwrapping the parcels.

Halloween is a big night around here. Main Street would be a fancy dress parade. There would be werewolves and ghouls, and rampant phantoms. There would be presidents and pop stars, sportsmen and actors, and people dressed as items of furniture. We would jostle with monsters, ghosts, skeletons, devils and the rest of the living. We would join clowns and bearded ladies, and a calf with two heads. Random quirks of nature and manufactured frauds: they all look alike in the end. We would become part of the stream of consciousness flowing down Main Street: a seething mass from this world and the next, come to party the night away. Everyone going for it. Everyone going somewhere, anywhere. Everyone pretending to be someone else.

Like every year, we would put a 'Closed' sign on the door and give Steve the night off. The question was, 'What costume do we wear?' and the answer had become, 'The same one as last year.' It was a lot cheaper. This came in for criticism. Our friends recognized us. People said it wasn't playing the game: the point was not to be recognized, at least not at a hundred paces. So, this year, we thought we'd change things around.

I remembered an old campaign badge from when Eugene McCarthy was running for the Democratic nomination: 'McCarthy! McCarthy? McCarthy.' That had always tickled me, but then I was an English teacher. I didn't see how we could impersonate a full stop. However, an exclamation mark and a question mark would be fun. Also appropriate, I thought at the time. Right now, a full stop seemed more to be desired.

Marcie knew a dressmaker who said she'd stitch some sheets round wire frames. Black stockings and white shoes would complete the effect. Slits and holes for eyes and mouths. No one would know who the hell we were. Now, this cornucopia of costumes lay spread on the table before me.

'Come on,' said Marcie; 'let's try them on.'

'Wait,' I said. 'I've got something to ask you first. Please will you take me to Colorado with you next summer.'

Marcie was taken aback for a moment.

'Of course I will,' she said. 'What's brought this on?'

'Nothing in particular,' I said.

15

We had a ball at Halloween. It was one of the best ever. Gazing down at the throng on Main Street from the balcony of the de Ritter hotel, it seemed that a good part of town must have come. Looked like a bunch of kids had run riot with the dressing-up box. This was the night when people could be anything they wanted to be. They could also do it any other night, I suppose, but this night it was permitted. In fact, it was expected. All the ambiguities of the world were on show. All its joys. Somewhere beneath, out of sight, all its sorrows too.

Marcie and I had a few drinks at the hotel, then went out to join the crowd. Took us a while to get used to walking in our costumes, aligning our eyes with the slits. I tripped over a kerbstone early on, and a guy dressed as the Statue of Liberty had to help me up. As you would. We watched the moon play hide-and-go-seek with the leaves of a tree, first transfixing the revellers with its glow, then plunging them into darkness. There was no telling where the next chance of light would strike, what tableau it would illumine, or what pose it would catch.

All you could be sure of was that, a moment or two later, it would be something different.

We thought we'd conceal our identities completely. We talked to people we knew in Mickey Mouse voices, to see if they recognized us. No one did, except for Steve, and he knew what costumes we'd got. We talked to Arlene and Franky. Arlene looked as if she was meant to be Elizabeth Taylor, which wasn't much of a stretch for her. I had a feeling she wouldn't come in anything that hid her looks. We thought she'd kitted Franky out as Errol Flynn. It was hard to be sure. He was wearing a neckerchief, leather jerkin and fancy pants, flashing a cutlass at anyone who came too close. They made a fine pair, damn them.

At one point, a group of guys dressed as Union soldiers ran into a group of guys dressed as Confederates. That could have got nasty. Nothing like fighting old battles, especially when the issues have never been resolved. Another guy was dressed up as the bastard town next door. I appreciate that you can't actually dress up as a town, but he had the name of the town on his head and his body appeared to be consumed with flames. You see, I'm not the only one round here to bear a grudge.

The town clock struck midnight. With a thousand other people, we swayed and surged up Main Street in a collective danse macabre. We coagulated outside the town hall for a last hurrah, alive to the night, dead to the world, and mostly dead drunk, so far as I could tell.

Then, two by two, couples slipped off into the fluorescent darkness, like into the last red sunset in a Western movie. Later, we'd take off the masks we'd worn for the occasion, pack them away, and put on our usual masks the next morning.

Well past midnight, the party over, we began to stroll home, arms around each other like they hadn't been in a while. We were about halfway back when we saw an apparition. On a bench, alone, sat a woman. She looked like she had been Ginger Rogers earlier in the evening. As we got closer, we could see that it was Mrs Riessen. She was in tears. Rouge and mascara streaked her face. She was running fingers through her hair, and it was a mess. We went over to her, took off the tops of our costumes and reminded her who we were.

'Can we help you in any way?' I asked.

'No, it's all right, thank you. I'll be fine.'

'You don't look fine,' Marcie said. 'Can we walk you home?'

'Thank you. Please don't trouble yourselves,' said Mrs Riessen. 'I'll be all right in a moment. I've had a nasty shock, that's all.'

'At the parade?'

'No. A little beforehand. It upset me rather. It was silly of me to have come, really. But I'd been so looking forward to it, and I'd got my costume and everything. I came with a friend, but she became ill and went home. I thought I'd be able to manage.'

'What upset you?' I asked.

'It's a private matter,' said Mrs Riessen. 'To do with family. A man came to see me and asked all sorts of impertinent questions. About my husband, and other things. It was very distressing. I really don't know what to make of it all.'

'Are you sure we can't walk with you to Pine?' asked Marcie. 'It's not far out of our way.'

'Well, if you're sure it wouldn't be any trouble, that would be very kind. I don't like being out on my own at this hour.'

So we walked Mrs Riessen home, and she thanked us, and we thanked her for giving us shelter the previous Sunday. Then we headed homewards ourselves.

'I guess that was Franky,' Marcie said.

'What good does he think that's going to do Arlene? She'd be furious if she knew.'

'Depends what he found out,' said Marcie.

I'd told Marcie about Franky's visit the previous day, and about our conversation. Well, I'd told her a quarter of the conversation: what Franky had said about Riessen and Jack and his engagement to Arlene. And that Franky was planning for them to live in Mr Hammond's house. You could say that a lead balloon would have felt like helium after that announcement.

Just after seven o'clock the next evening, Franky and Arlene bounced into the bar, a few minutes apart. Franky swaggered in like he'd won the state lottery. Marcie may have been right that his charm had a sell-by date of five minutes, but the five minutes were metaphorical. They had already extended to several weeks, with bookings likely to be confirmed for a further season. Possibly for a lifetime. Arlene looked jubilant too, triumphal even. It seemed like they were in honeymoon mode already. Arlene stared up at Franky as if he was her hero, and Franky pretended not to notice, as if he got that look regularly.

I haven't given much impression of the passion between Franky and Arlene, because they mostly kept it private, which was decorous if disappointing. You could sense it, though. You mightn't get to see the film, but the trailer played in the bar room each night they were there. Some nights, the trailer was short: the two of them had barely met up before they left again, pawing each other like kittens. It was nothing like how Arlene had been with Davy. I handed Arlene her cocktail and was about to pour a beer for Franky, when he stopped me.

'Save it for later,' he said. 'I need to do something at home. Look after Arlene for a while, won't you? Don't do it too good, mind.'

Sounded like he was about to take Arlene to their new home later that night. Maybe he'd gone to put the champagne on ice. I tried not to think about it and turned my attention to Arlene.

'You're looking good tonight,' I said. 'I mean, especially good.'

'Why, thank you,' said Arlene. 'I'm feeling great.'

'Did you enjoy Halloween?'

'I loved Halloween. It was fabulous. Worth waiting for all these years. Were you there?'

'You bet we were.'

'I didn't see you. There was such a crowd. Franky and I went as Elizabeth Taylor and Clark Gable.'

'We thought he was Errol Flynn,' I said.

'No. Clark Gable. You saw us?'

'We talked to you.'

'You did what? I don't remember that. How were you dressed?'

'I was an exclamation mark, and Marcie was a question mark,' I said.

'So that was you!' said Arlene. 'You were in those white sheets. You meanies. You put on silly voices. I hope we didn't say anything bad. We thought you were the Ku Klux Klan.'

'Your grasp of punctuation is poor,' I said. 'Tell me why you're feeling so good.'

'You remember that night when Franky first came in the bar? I said I wanted a twenty-four-carat, rock-solid hero, and Marcie said that Franky wasn't the one. Well, she was wrong. Franky is Batman and Superman and Captain America rolled into one. He's the hero to end all heroes.'

Marcie was standing a few feet away from me at the time, talking to someone else. It didn't stop her hearing.

Wisely, she decided not to comment, and satisfied herself with the raise of an eyebrow.

'What's he done to deserve that notice?' I asked.

'He's such a wonderful man,' said Arlene, 'and he did such a wonderful thing. He found out about Jack for me. Would you believe it? And then this morning, I found out for myself.'

'You did? You met him?'

'No,' said Arlene. 'I discovered all about him in a newspaper piece. Wait till you hear it. You'll be so surprised!'

'About what?'

'I can't say now. I must tell Franky first. But I'll tell you soon.'

'Is Jack alive?'

'No,' said Arlene. 'He's dead. But at least I know who he was.'

'And who was he?'

'That's complicated.' Those were the same words Franky had used when I'd asked him about Hammond's house. 'There may be money involved. Quite a lot of money, I think. Why do things always turn out complicated?'

'Because they are,' Marcie would have said. In fact, I could hear her saying it under her breath at that moment. I hope the other customer didn't think she was listening to him.

'Stop being mysterious,' I said. 'It can't be that complicated. Why don't you tell me?'

'Not till I've told Franky.'

'You will be careful, Arlene, won't you?'

'Careful of what? Of Franky?'

'Amongst other things.'

Arlene reached over and tweaked my nose. 'You're jealous,' she said. 'You and Marcie can say what you like about Franky, but he's a generous man. Look what he gave me.'

She stretched out her hand. A large ring adorned her finger. Could have been diamond. Could have been paste. I don't know enough to say. Either way, it was an engagement ring. It didn't give me a good feeling. I felt my hard-earned cash had paid for it.

'Come into some money, has he?'

Arlene smiled. 'As a matter of fact, he has. And a house. In fact, we're going to be living there. You really are jealous, aren't you?'

I let that one go. I was beyond jealousy where Franky was concerned. But I was feeling mad at him. Mad that my stolen money was being flashed around the bar. Mad that it now looked as if we'd got Franky as a long-term neighbour. I'd had enough.

'Have you seen Franky's house?' I asked. 'Do you know where it is?'

'No,' said Arlene. 'He's taking me there tonight.'

'Just be careful, Arlene.'

'What's there to be careful about?'

'Just be careful.'

She got up from the stool and paced around the room. I think I'd unsettled her, which was the intention. Over at the window, she looked into the parking lot.

'Franky's car is there,' she said when she returned.

'That's strange,' I said. 'He usually parks it round the back.'

'Not when I'm with him,' said Arlene. 'And not tonight. Why would he park it round the back? And why is it here at all? He said he'd gone to do something at home. Why hasn't he taken the car?'

Should I tell Arlene? Why shouldn't I tell Arlene?

'Look,' I said. 'Franky's house is Mr Hamond's house. He's been living there for about three months now. Technically, I suppose he's squatting, but it's more than that. He's doing the place up. He's making it into a proper home. For you, it would appear.'

'What? Are you sure?' Anxiety was replacing the exuberance.

'Quite sure. I went with him when he first looked inside the house. Davy came too. It was after the visit that Franky decided he'd take the place over. He didn't want anyone to know, so he's left the front gates bolted and uses our parking lot to get in and out.'

Arlene said nothing. She looked disconcerted.

'That's not all,' I said. 'What's Franky's surname? Do you know?'

'Albertino,' said Arlene.

'Not anymore, it isn't. He changed it to Hammond when he moved into the house. Changed it officially, I mean.'

'Are you sure of that?'

'Yes.'

'Why would he want to do that, change his name?'

'I should think it's either a scam to make him look like the legal owner . . .' I paused. I wasn't sure if I should mention the other alternative. Arlene could figure it out for herself.

'. . . or?'

I think she wanted me to say it for her.

'Or he's Mr Hammond's son. That's my take on it, for what it's worth.'

Arlene looked like she'd been poleaxed. She scrunched up her fingers and closed her eyes tight shut. She was breathing heavily. She said nothing.

Then she stood bolt upright, walked over to the window and looked out of it for a while. She was calmer when she came back to the bar.

'No, he isn't,' she said. 'He can't be.'

'How come you're so sure of that?'

Arlene exploded. 'Because you're lying to me, you shithead!' she shouted.

Marcie was standing by my side now. Arlene was silent, her brow clouded, her mouth pursed. She was breathing even more heavily.

'Arlene,' I said, 'talk to us. For once in your life, open

up. Don't be afraid of telling people things. We want to help you.'

'No,' she said. 'Not now. Not ever.' She stared at us. 'Bastard. Bastard.'

She was now incredibly angry. I had never seen her angry.

'What's the problem, Arlene?'

'You're the problem, you bastard!' she screamed at me. 'How can you stand there and say that Franky is Mr Hammond's son. Have you any idea what you're saying? As for you –' she turned toward Marcie – 'I know you hate him. Franky's told me the lies you've spread about him. Now you stand there and tell me that you want to help me. You don't give a shit, the pair of you.'

Her face was red, her hands shaking. I was going to speak, but was stopped by the reappearance of Franky.

'What's up, sugar?'

'This man,' she said. 'These people. They think that Mr Hammond was your father.'

Franky looked at us. Then he looked at Arlene and smiled.

'He was,' he said. 'I was going to tell you when we got to the house.'

'No!' screamed Arlene. Tears were streaming down her face now. 'No! No! No! He isn't. He can't be.'

'Why not?' asked Franky.

'He mustn't be. Don't you understand?'

Arlene was shouting at the top of her voice. The bar

was full that night. All other conversations stopped. All eyes were fixed on Arlene.

Then the anger subsided. Her shoulders sagged. She sat down on a stool, her stool, put her head in her hands and began to sob.

'No,' she said in a whisper. 'Of course you don't understand. I haven't told you yet. How could you understand?'

Franky had been watching Arlene with a look of bewilderment, like he couldn't begin to guess what lay behind this outburst. I don't think he was acting.

'Told me what?' he said.

Arlene got to her feet and wiped her cheeks on her sleeve. She stood very still for a moment. Then she took Franky by the arm and led him slowly out of the bar.

Franky freed his arm and tried to put it round Arlene, but she pushed it gently away. They both turned their heads back toward us.

'So long, Steve,' said Franky. 'Good to have met you.'

No farewell to Marcie or me; just to a guy he barely knew. They were the last words I heard him speak. Arlene didn't say anything as she shook her head slowly from side to side.

I'm truly sorry that this should have been my last memory of Arlene. It was ineffably sad.

I don't think she meant what she said to us. I don't think that her reaction had anything to do with me, intrinsically. She would have learned what I told her a few hours later in any case. I happened to be the Western Union guy. She wasn't angry with me for telling her that Franky was Hammond's son. She was furious with the information itself.

That was Marcie's take on it too. Marcie felt that Arlene had suddenly understood something, everything. We didn't know what Arlene knew, so we couldn't make the connection that she made. Or not till later, anyhow.

I watched them through the bar room window, standing opposite each other in the parking lot, close to each other. It was too far to hear what was being said. I guess they were talking softly, and our double glazing was too good. We could see though, because the lot was illuminated. We watched two silhouettes act out a mime show.

It was Arlene who did the talking. She seemed to be explaining something to Franky. It took a while. Then she produced something from her purse and unfolded it. It was large, like a sheet of newspaper. She showed it to Franky, standing back a little, leaving him his own space to read it. Franky seemed to be struggling with the information it contained. He read it, then put the paper to his side, then read it again. He looked at Arlene and shook his head. They were both crying.

Marcie was standing at the window with me. These were not the people we knew out there. We were watching two strangers. I thought of how I'd recognized Franky that first time I'd seen him when he came back, how I'd recognized him by his essence. That essence had now

261

deserted him. If I hadn't known it was Franky standing there, I'm not sure I would have guessed. I'm not sure I would have guessed it was Arlene either. Her essence had deserted her also. What remained were two husks, talking to each other.

I felt like a voyeur watching this spectacle. Hard to remember, but this was a private tragedy, whatever its nature, not a public performance for our benefit. I should have gone back to the bar, but I couldn't drag myself away.

After a while, the talking ended. They stood there, an inch apart, but apart. There was a gentleness, a tenderness, in their manner. Franky moved tentatively to put his arms around Arlene, seemingly unsure whether she would accept the gesture. She did. They stood there for several minutes, neck to neck, hugging. Then Arlene broke gently off, walked toward her car and drove away. No backward glance.

Franky stood there a while longer, still in tears. I expected him to return to his house of broken dreams. He did not. He got into his Mustang and roared off into the night.

16

I think life is sad (Arlene said to me once). Don't you? I think life is so very sad. All I want to do, all I've ever wanted to do, is to reach out and touch the world with kindness. The world will not be touched in that way. It doesn't want kindness. It needs it, but it doesn't want it. And the thing is that I can't touch myself with kindness either. I need it, but I don't want it. I'm not worthy of it. None of us is worthy of it.

I wait (Arlene said) for one transcending moment. I wait for the moment that will make sense of every other moment, that will make sense of me. I don't think I make sense, do you? I don't think any of us makes sense. We wander round with no great idea of who we are or what we're doing. We think we know, sometimes. Then we do something we'd never do, or say something we'd never say, so we don't know at all.

Who are you? (This question was addressed to me.) Who are you? You're a guy who keeps a bar. That much I know. I don't know a whole heap else. I suppose I know that you're even tempered, that you don't fuss about things much. I suppose I know that you're in love with Marcie, or at least rub along with Marcie.

You're a stranger, really: a familiar stranger. As I'm a familiar stranger to you, I imagine. Humans aren't much good at accepting that, especially if they're shacked up with each other. They think they ought to know each other absolutely. They think it's a failing if they don't. My point (Arlene said) is that it's not a failing, nor a surprise. It doesn't speak about the quality of the love. If we are strangers to ourselves, how can other people not be strangers to us? If we've lived these years inside our own skin, with only a vague idea of what that means, how can we ever be inside the skin of another?

I expect you think I'm crazy, don't you? Most people do. That's because they don't understand me (said Arlene). I don't understand them either, so I'm not in a position to make an issue of it, but I wish they wouldn't judge me so. An end to judgements, I say. We don't know enough about anyone to make them. I don't make judgements about you. Well, I do, I suppose. I judge you as a bartender. That's because I've had a lot of experience of bartenders, so I know what I'm talking about. You're pretty good, by the way. I don't judge you in any other respect. I may judge your actions, but I don't judge you.

The fact is that we live selfish lives. We're not interested in other people, unless they make us feel better in some way, like they love us, or they pay us, or they amuse us. People tell me that's cynical. I plead guilty to cynicism, but I don't rate it as a charge. When I was young, I was not a cynic and I had illusions. Then I ditched the illusions and became a cynic. That's the worst of both worlds, if you ask me. So I decided to keep the cynicism, and bring back the illusions. That works best for me. I like illusions now. Illusions are another way of looking at the truth. If we can't be sure that our truths do not deceive us, how can we be sure that our illusions do?

I used to get taken to church when I was young. The minister told us that, if we wanted to be forgiven, we should cast out sin. I asked him how, if I cast out sin, I would have anything for which I needed to be forgiven. He didn't know the answer to that. Forgiveness is a parasite. It feeds upon the host of sin. Redemption is a parasite. It feeds upon the host of a fall. Likewise, illusion is a parasite upon reality, and the other way about. They're symbiotic. If you can't define reality, how can you define illusion? They're different facets of the same thing.

Yes, I like my illusions (said Arlene). And sometimes one of them becomes a reality. I think I should be going now. It doesn't matter where I go. I go where I go. I come from where I come from. As you do; as we all do. I'm happy to come from Pittsburgh, if it helps you to feel you know me. I don't see what difference it makes.

Arlene left town after her conversation with Franky. We wouldn't see her again. Not that we knew that, for a while. Her appearances had always been irregular. Knowing when to give up on Arlene was like knowing when to give up on someone lost at sea. Common sense says you should give up early, but you don't. Something unexpected may have happened. Pirates capture you, or a mermaid flips you on her tail. You never know. I haven't had what anyone would call an eventful life. Nothing much has happened out of the ordinary. I don't know what will happen tomorrow.

It took more than five months to give up on Arlene. It was Marcie who called time on the hoping.

'Oh, for God's sake, boys,' she said one April evening. 'Stop looking at that goddam door every time it flaps. It's not her. She's not coming back. We've seen the last of her.'

That sort of gave us permission to discuss her. To discuss her in the past tense, I mean. Till then it had been present tense, as if our relationship with her was in hiatus. Now we were refining words for the post-mortem. Not that we thought she was dead, just dead to us. Which amounted to the same thing.

'We never knew a darned thing about her, did we?' said Steve.

'Oh, I don't agree with that,' said Marcie. 'I think we knew a lot.'

'Like what?' I asked.

'Like she was lonely,' said Marcie. 'Like she hadn't been used to love. Like she wanted to be appreciated. Like she'd had a tough life. Like she needed to trust someone. Like she never gave up hoping.'

'I don't call that a lot,' said Mike.

'I call it as much as any of us knows about anyone,' Marcie said.

I walked over to the jukebox. A retrospective on Arlene didn't seem complete without listening to 'My Guy'. I played it once and a clicking ran across the song, so I played it again. The second time around, the record started jumping. I thought there must be some dirt in the grooves. I opened the machine and took the disc out. It was cracked. I don't know how. I broke it in half and threw it in the bin.

In the end, we are alone. It's how we arrive and it's how we depart. The journey between is little more than pulling tattered fabric about us as protection from the chill of the high lonesome. I have no complaints, but somewhere I've been missing the point. Most of us have been missing the point. There are so many things that aren't right in the world, and never have been right. I was going to say, 'And never will be right,' but I'm not that big a pessimist.

Arlene could have said that. Except for the last part. She is that big a pessimist, or was. Would I have said it before I met her? I don't know. Small threads of Arlene's tattered fabric rubbing off on me; small threads of mine rubbing off on her. Point zero zero one degree of frost removed from both our lives. She fretted that she was not original. I reckon that was the one thing she was. Not that it matters greatly now, if it ever did.

I was on the road a few days later, thinking about Arlene and Franky. We hadn't seen Franky again either, but I'd heard from him. Back in January, a letter had arrived, postmarked Omaha. It contained a cheque for two thousand, eight hundred and thirty-six dollars, nothing else. I expected the cheque to bounce, but it didn't. In the end, Franky must have cared a little for other people's opinion of him, or at least for my opinion. Arlene didn't care for anyone's opinion. I'm not sure that's true, actually. Maybe Arlene cared too much and didn't want to let it show.

I thought of the cracked record, of the things in her life, in the lives of all of us, that were cracked or broken. It had felt like the end of an era. A short era, as eras go, but not short on incident. Arlene defined the era for me. I imagine Franky defined it for Marcie. Let's be even-handed and say that the era belonged to both of them.

I was driving along small roads to a neighbouring town, fifty miles away. I don't like going that far, but I needed to get a pump fixed, and that was the nearest place that could do it fast. I had left early in the morning, with the hope of being back by lunchtime. It was a pretty town, with old houses running along Main Street, and a bridge over a river. I found the repair shop easily enough, in a back street. They said the pump would take an hour to fix. There was a café nearby, so I thought I'd wait there. The local newspaper was lying on the table, and I leafed through it as I drank a coffee.

That's when I saw the article.

It stated that a woman had drowned in the town last Tuesday, rescuing a child from the swollen river, near the bridge. The child, a little girl, had survived. The woman wasn't believed to be local. It was a long piece, telling two stories, undecided which was the more interesting, toggling between the two. One story was the selfless act of a stranger, risking her life, and in the end giving it, for the sake of a child. I don't want to sound mean, but I'm glad it wasn't a dog. When people drown trying to save a dog, I find it dispiriting. This was uplifting, in its sad way.

The other story was the mystery of the saviour. Little was known about her for certain, according to the paper.

Except that she had black hair, and was probably in her late thirties.

And was thought to have come from Pittsburgh.

And that her name was thought to be Arlene Mitchell.

I put my face into my hands and wept. Poor, lost Arlene. Who wanted to do something unique and be remembered for it. We would have remembered her always. In any event.

The scant pieces of information about Arlene had been culled from a conversation between her and a barman, just before the accident. He ran a place near the bridge, the paper said. He had been the sole witness to the event, apart from the mother. He was the one who had called the emergency services. The paper didn't give his name. His information about Arlene was relayed to the world by a police source. He sounded keen to be kept out of the story. There was a long quote from the child's mother, overwhelmed equally with relief at her daughter's rescue and grief at the death of the rescuer.

It was a weekly newspaper and the drowning had happened the previous week, six days before the paper was published. Six days. Plenty of time for the police to have discovered more. It seemed all they'd found was a left shoe. That was where they got the name Mitchell. It was written inside the shoe.

The article listed what they had failed to find. No purse. No purse? What woman doesn't carry a purse? Arlene always did when I'd seen her. No address. No one, apart from the barman, to come forward with an identification. No mention of a black sports car. No photo of her. I imagine they wouldn't print one of a dead woman, and that was the only photo they would have had. The report said that the police had circulated a description.

Arlene had achieved something extraordinary. We come with tags, like we are dogs, or combatants in a war. All manner of everyday items leave a trail as to who we are: trails that lead to bank accounts, to friends and family, to addresses, to cars, to insurance companies, to secrets. Closed-circuit cameras track our movements. Each of us is somebody else's business. Except for Arlene. She was nobody's business but her own. So what to do about the burial of someone with no apparent existence, with no money to pay for a funeral, with no known next of kin? The paper announced there was to be a service at two o'clock that afternoon, at a church on the edge of town. I ordered another coffee and mulled things over.

What should I do? I could have telephoned someone, but there was no point. No one except Marcie might have wanted to attend the service. I had the car, so she wouldn't have been able to come. I would tell her later what had happened, face to face, and she would cry too. I didn't want to burden Davy with the news; didn't know how he might react, or Mary-Jane. I didn't know how to contact Franky, and wouldn't if I could. I might have contacted the police, but I knew little more than they knew already. I'd known it for longer; not in any more detail. So I thought I'd hang around for a while and go to the service on my own, to say a collective goodbye from all of us.

I picked up the pump and put it in the car, then walked toward the river, toward the bridge. On the way, I bought my own copy of the local paper. When I reached the spot, I stared into the water, where it rushed beneath the bridge, and wanted to hurl myself into it. I began to imagine what had happened, but I had to turn away.

I went in search of the barman in the story. There was only one bar by the bridge, and only one man behind the counter. The right man, as it turned out. I explained why I'd come.

'Did you know her?' he asked.

'Yes,' I said. 'I keep a bar too. Fifty miles away. I knew her well. Arlene was a regular.'

'Not anymore she isn't.' I thought that was a graceless remark. Maybe I was being oversensitive.

'Can you tell me anything else? Apart from what's in the paper?'

'I could,' said the man. 'I don't know that I will. I prefer to mind my own business. Don't go round talking to newspapermen and cops.'

'I'm neither of those.'

'Everyone's snooping around,' he said. 'I had a guy from the IRS in here a while ago.'

'When was that?' I asked.

'Oh, I don't know. Tail end of last year. October, November maybe. I've had enough of it. I'm trying to run a bar.'

'I'm not from the Revenue either,' I said. 'I was a friend of hers. I want to know what happened. So will other people.'

There was a pause while the barman scratched his testicles. Then he decided to open up a little, by his own limited standards. I was glad I didn't drink in his bar. Everyone knows that a good barman can't afford to mind his own business.

'Not much more I can tell you,' he said. 'She came in late that afternoon. About four-thirty, I'd say.'

'On her own?'

'Yup. On her own. She ordered a vodka Martini. I told

her we didn't do those, so she had a vodka and Coke. She was half cut already, if you ask me. She sat up here at the bar, right where you're sitting, and started waving a newspaper around and asking me about someone who used to live in town. She was rambling most of the time and I was only half listening. I get too many strangers coming in here with hard-luck stories.'

'Were you able to answer the questions?'

'I don't know,' said the barman. 'Maybe. She was going on about someone called Jack. Died about three years ago. She asked if anyone called Jack used to drink here. What sort of a question's that? As a matter of fact, there was a Jack who used to come in here sometimes.'

'Did he have a surname?'

'Several, it seemed. She thought the one she was looking for was Jack Dulap.'

'Dulap?'

'Yup,' said the barman. 'Dulap. Mind you, he seems to have gone by quite a lot of names, so who knows. If it was the same guy, I knew him only as Jack.'

'Was it the same guy?'

'Hard to say. The lady didn't seem to know much about him.'

'What was he like?' I asked. 'The Jack that used to come in here.'

'Tall. Little pencil moustache. Good-looking guy. A character.'

'Age?'

'Well, he didn't come in often, but he came in over many years. Last time I saw him, I guess he was mid-sixties, maybe seventy.'

'And when was that?'

'Oh, a few years ago now.'

'Sounds like Arlene's Jack,' I said.

'If you say so. I wouldn't know. I don't think the lady was too sure herself.'

'What other questions did she ask?'

'Wanted to know where he lived. I think she hoped to go visit the place. I wasn't able to help her with that. I've no idea where he lived.'

'How did she come across?' I asked. 'Did she seem happy?'

'I'd say she was unhappy as hell,' said the barman. 'She must have been a good-looking woman once, but she'd let herself go. And she was the worse for drink, like I said. She asked me if I knew what it was like to have your world fall to pieces. Cheerful sort of question. I said I didn't.'

'What else did she say?'

'Jeez. I'm not Mr Memory Man. Besides, she talked in a way that made it hard to understand what she was saying. I sort of lost interest, to be honest.'

'But she told you her name was Arlene?'

'Yup. Told me that when she arrived. Stretched her hand across the counter to shake my hand and said her name was Arlene.'

'And that she came from Pittsburgh?'

'I think it was Pittsburgh. I could tell she wasn't local, so I asked. It was someplace beginning with P. Could have been Philadelphia.'

'When the little girl fell in the river,' I said. 'What happened then?'

'We heard these shrieks outside, from the riverbank. The lady picked up her purse . . .'

'. . . her purse? The police said they hadn't found a purse.'

'Look,' he said, 'I'm telling you what I know. She had a purse with her. She must have taken it with her to the river. If so, the cops likely wouldn't have found it. Water flows swiftly under that bridge. Anyhow, she picked up her purse and rushed out. You know the rest. I would have gone myself, but . . . Well, you know how it is.'

I felt that this stone had yielded all the blood it had to offer. I settled up and contemplated whether to leave a decent tip. I decided in favour of no tip. I was mad at the guy for not going to Arlene's assistance.

'Thanks for your help,' I said.

'Yeah, well, don't come asking for more.'

It was now lunchtime, but I didn't feel like eating. There was an hour to the service, so I strolled around town in the April sunshine, thinking of Arlene, making sure I had it straight in my head, or as straight as it could be.

I wondered what Arlene had done in those few

months since she left us; where she had gone. They hadn't been happy times, for sure. Arlene had never looked less than immaculate when I saw her. What she discovered that last day in our town, what was in that newspaper, what she told Franky in my parking lot, had knocked her sideways. Maybe it knocked Franky the same way.

If it was what I now suspected, it would knock anyone sideways.

In the end, Arlene had gone back to doing the one thing she knew how to do: looking for Jack. She'd spent so much time looking for Jack, wondering about Jack, asking about Jack. And though she now knew who he was, and some of what he'd done, he was as opaque to her as he had been in the beginning. And dead, of course. But that hadn't stopped the quest. A new day. A new town. One more barman to ask questions of. Once again, the answers had failed to satisfy: even the parts that turned out to be true could not be trusted to be true. No matter. There would be another day. Another town. Except there wasn't.

The saddest thing was that I think she and Franky could have been happy together. She'd have had a lot to put up with, and so would he. There would have been a large part of Arlene he could never reach, but that elusiveness would have kept him interested. One thing you couldn't do with Arlene was to chew her up and spit her out, at least not without chewing up and spitting out a large part of yourself. That might have come as a novelty for Franky.

You spend your life searching for something, for someone, and when you find it, you wish you hadn't.

It was a small church, hidden away, property of the First Presbyterians. A police officer stood outside the door, respectful and alert at the same time, eyes alternately cast down and scanning new arrivals for who they might be and what they might know. She approached me as I came to the door, enquired whether I'd been personally acquainted with the deceased. I didn't want to get into that. I said I lived locally and had come to pay my respects. That was about as true as anything in life. She took my name and address all the same. We weren't the only ones piecing things together.

The service was about to start as I walked inside. The coffin was there: a plain wooden box on a trestle. There was a single bunch of flowers upon it. Perhaps a bouquet of gratitude from the town for an anonymous saviour, or from the family whose integrity was thereby preserved.

There were a handful of people in the church: a dozen at the most. In the old days, families paid professional mourners to attend, extravagant in their grief, trying to trick God into believing that the deceased was popular, beloved of all, deserving of a place in heaven. If I believed in God, I don't think I'd believe in one that was so easily taken in. Here was someone who deserved tears. Few came to shed them. Arlene had been a local heroine, but just for one day, and that day was last week. Time had been called on her fifteen minutes of fame. No one much turned up from town to remember the stranger who had saved the life of a child.

Before finding a pew, I looked around to see if I recognized anyone in the congregation. It didn't seem likely. I half wondered whether Franky might have come. There was no sign of him. There was no one that I knew.

In the front pew was a woman of about thirty-five, soberly dressed, unremarkable. With her was a girl of five or so, no doubt her daughter. I made the obvious assumption. I expect it was correct, although it might not have been. They turned their heads to look at me, and turned them again as soon as their eyes met mine. I sat at the back, next to the aisle, prepared for an exit.

I wondered what had become of the young girl's father. Separated or divorced, hundreds of miles away, unaware of one tragedy, or the closeness of another? Perhaps not knowing that he had a daughter. Or none of those things. Maybe at work that day, like every day, bringing home the bacon. 'I ain't got the time, Betsy. You go. You go with Loosie. That'll work fine. You can tell me about it after.'

Stumbling forward into what passes for a future, blindfold tight around the eyes, hands upon the shoulders of someone who feels like they know where they're going, but blindfolded also and walking around in figures of eight.

One summer's day, fourth of July, if Mrs Riessen was right, if that's when it really was, Jack Nightingale stepped out into the streets of one of his home towns, goodness knows which, or how many he had, careless of the possession of life, unencumbered by a sure identity. The flags would have been flying, the bunting stretched across the storefronts. Perhaps he thought he'd buy a bottle from the liquor store, to celebrate later, when the Indiana wife wasn't around. Or perhaps he didn't die in a liquor store. That could have been a lawyer's joke. If lawyers have jokes. Perhaps he did die in a brothel in Akron.

Wherever it was, a heart attack took Jack Nightingale out, along with Riessen, Dulap and Hammond, along with chunks of other people's lives, leaving question marks and stray children behind him.

When I had trod the dust in Mr Hammond's house and disturbed the rest of the years, I was not trampling on people, I thought. I was intrigued by a mystery, not by a misery. I was trampling just the same. Despite everything I'd learned, I still had no idea where Arlene had lived, how near our town, how far. She must have lived somewhere. In three, five, ten years' time, will someone else like me explore another abandoned domain, invent other explanations for the unknowable, while the locals say how the woman who lived there hadn't been seen for a while and kept herself to herself?

I like the idea of Arlene being with all those aliases for eternity. I think they belong together.

My mind drifted. I thought of the trees that guarded Mr Hammond's property. That guarded Mr Franky's property. The trees were trying to talk to me, but they had nothing to say. One of them looked like Arlene. She was one of the guardians of Mr Hammond's property.

Someone in the church whispered. The sound was the world, the entire world, reduced to a billionth billionth of its volume. The sound was everything that was being said or sung in the world at that moment, distilled to a fraction of a whisper. If my hearing had been good enough, my command of languages complete, I could have discriminated between each sound and known what the world was saying. Perhaps this is the sound that God hears. If he exists.

I didn't pay close attention to the pastor's words. He would know less about the woman he was burying than I did. He would know what she had done; could talk heroically of that. But he didn't know the woman who had done it, which came close to rendering his words meaningless, making impersonal the most personal of sacrifices. Without listening much, I knew his homily must be banal, because it could be nothing else. My thoughts had the movement of a cloud of hornets, but Arlene was always there amongst the stinging. I wondered if she had come from Pittsburgh. A strange thing to invent, if not, but no stranger than many other things about Arlene. Or maybe it was us that invented it.

I sensed the pastor was coming to the end of his oration, and I couldn't think what would come after, except goodbye and amen. It was time for me to go. I wanted to leave silently, but there's always a shiver of something to say we are here. At the noise of dust breaking, two heads turned and two pairs of eyes requested that I should stay. I was a stranger in the church. There were questions to be asked of me, responses to be given, and these were the essential intercessions of the day.

I couldn't stay. I'm sorry, but I could not stay. I had no answers for them, nor for anyone. I walked out of the door into the bleached sunlight, blinded by the glare of a great obscurity.